ACUPUNCTURE OF THE MIND

an experience by Goran Zivanovic

© Goran Zivanovic 2017

Published by

Gothic Zen Studios

AcupunctureOfTheMind.com

GothicZen.com.au

ISBN: 978-0-6481846-2-1

Acknowledgements

Clare, without you, who knows? You reached into my heart and soul to extract experiences that were turning into dust. You felt a pulse in my stories and gave these fading words a purposeful life. Thank you for showing me a way out of the mind traps by offering love, encouragement and patience.

To the homeless: Sandy, Paul, and many others, for their willingness to communicate and share their stories with me, the stranger.

My sincere gratitude goes towards religious spokespersons recorded anonymously within these pages. Although my questions were raw, your responses were well-received.

Thank you to those who physically died yesterday and gave me perspective today. Your worth is not lost within this time capsule of disturbing and uplifting revelations.

To you, the reader and experiencer, willing to take a risk by absorbing these challenging passages and trying to make sense of it in your personal reality.

Chapters

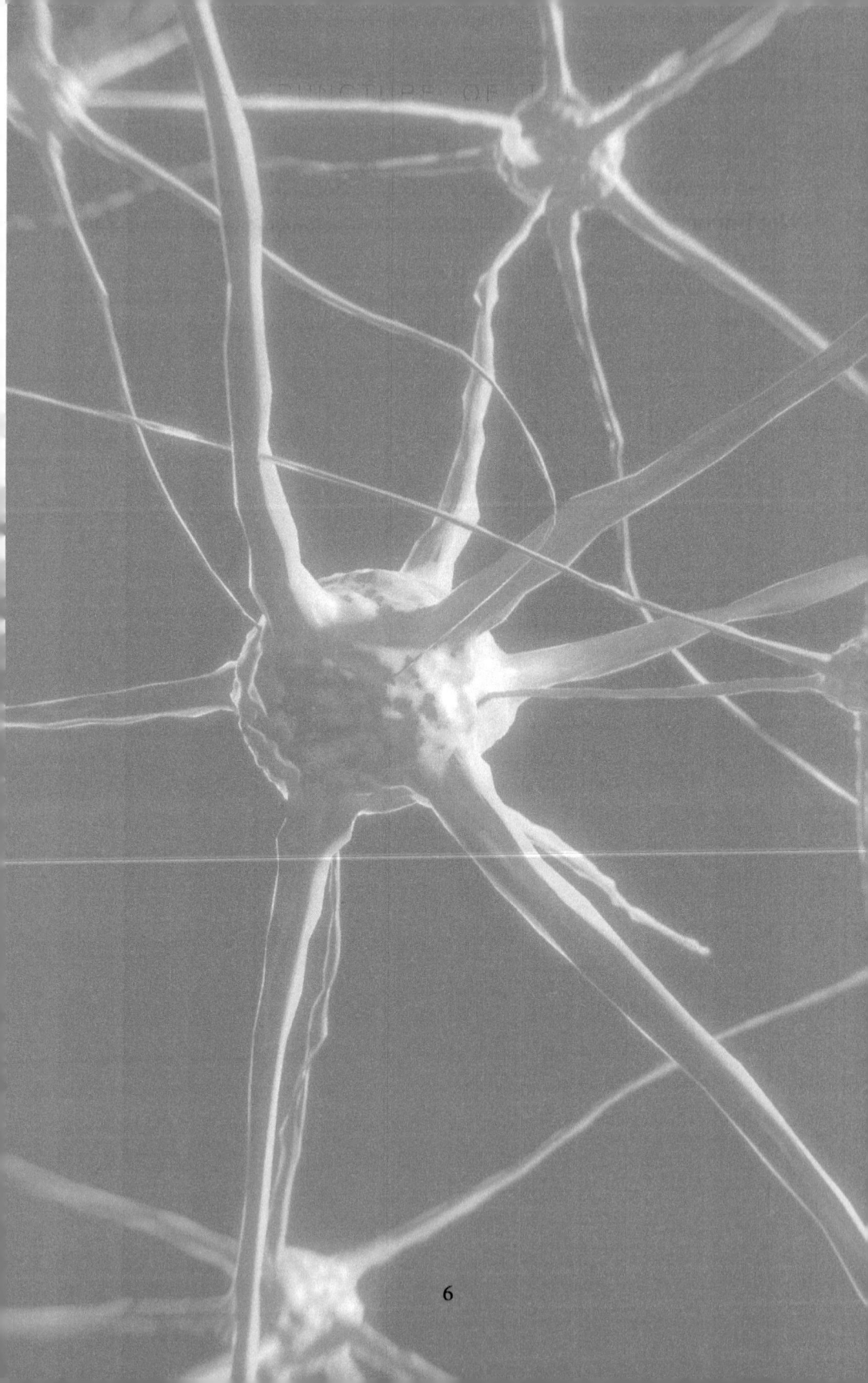

Introduction

My mind was full of doubt when I asked the cosmos for direction. I needed to construct a safe platform for you, the observer, to witness Julian's sharp lines, steep drop-offs, and disorientating worlds. The universe did not respond with a simple template. Instead, I was informed that authentic decision-making always comes from within, otherwise I will always be without.

Before I was born, Julian Aquinas Marcus entered a career in the priesthood. He became a dedicated preacher who served his God, church, and family. For two decades Father Julian spoke to those who were impoverished and without divine light. Ironically, it was through this pious calling that he emerged a bitterly marked man. He began to explore his personal identity whilst revisiting years of religious instruction. The furnace had a melting point and he kept adding more fuel to the chamber.

Something profound happened to Father Julian shortly before his shield of faith failed to protect him from apostate views. Ongoing encounters with a homeless man, whom he only referred to as 'G', left him conflicted. Every tree started to look the same in his Garden of

Eden, and every fruit tasted just as bitter as the next. The bible man then shouldered the heaviest burden ever known to a holy person: the concept of God without religion.

Julian began to write down his own observations, rather than adhere to someone else's interpretation of divine things. He found himself alone in a world of billions and appreciated the true meaning of homelessness. Being out of step with a society that could not feel his pain was a familiar experience, but all he could do was write in his journal to reconnect with Earth's gravity. That only got him so far until the next breakdown.

In an attempt to explore the secular self, Julian sought refuge in psychiatry, not as a patient, but as a mind specialist. This highly skilled position came circumvent and was full of controversy. As part of his religious duties, Julian had been trained in many disciplines of psychology and medicine. He was responsible for the mental welfare of his congregation and the 'lost sheep', whom he tried to convert. The overarching purpose of his quasi-psychological practices was for the benefit of the Seven Safe Religions, his employer at the time, and less so for his flock.

There were conflicts in his new role as a fully fledged mind specialist. He detested being called 'Professor' or any other official title that gave the impression of higher authority. Julian refused to practice certain textbook laws and often led the sessions with charming arrogance, instead of a methodical process. He pushed further into an area of the brain where few professionals dared to explore. Parapsychology was commonplace and anomalies were ever-present on his couch.

Psychiatric wards are full of mirrors. During his mind surgeries, Julian practiced healing methods unlike I, his long-time colleague, had ever known. My time at Cathedral Psychiatric Clinic is where my reevaluating and growth took shape. At present, I am one of the Directors of Psychiatry at Cathedral.

'Death fertilises rebirth,' Julian reminded me often. 'It's only natural.' Something within Julian died long ago – I regularly saw the shadowy remains lodged deep in his eyes – and what lingered was the fertilisation of a creature few individuals will ever recognise. 'In a lifetime we constantly die and rebirth,' he insisted. 'Despite this, only a fraction of people will seek a different climate to re-establish themselves. Growth is restricted for the frightened, root-bound ones.'

Julian's thought process was intoxicating. Increasingly, I felt it was my responsibility to water the harvest and allow the public to sample his philosophies; to distribute the genius within this crumbling madness.

I cannot verify all the content in Julian's manuscript, which consists of unsubstantiated moments inside and outside the walls of Cathedral Psychiatric Clinic. His biographical accounts might further infect your psychological wounds, or they could heal your bites. I will navigate you through the uneasy movements of his world, and allow you to steer these events to your own destination.

Julian allowed me to understand the concept of death from a non-clinical viewpoint, and it somehow belongs in the field of psychological science. You will judge Julian when he enters you in his quest to understand the depths of your actions. He can be extremely vague at times, until logic surfaces and stings you with needle-sharp precision. Distress is imminent when he highlights what we have become. He tested my spirit a few times by whispering my name in an empty room.

'Bleedthrough' is Julian's Mona Lisa – a speculative piece of art, an obsession, and the only true reflection of his self worth. It is something that never completely satisfied the man because it fails perfection, and that's also its appeal. Even when we put these words to rest, his Bleedthrough will survive, because time is only the length between our birth and death.

Much like the God some of us fear and love, you could become all too consumed by Julian's interpretations of our existence. You might begin to search for signs of wonder that may, or may not, exist. Search, but don't tell anyone you found the answers here, because everyone has a different question to ask.

Great people enter this world through all variety of women. I did not know my mentor's mother; however, as a woman, I revere her for bearing a son by the name of Julian Aquinas Marcus.

My name is Bliss Stone, and these insights into Julian's convictions are made public at his request. I cannot deny the kindred spirit we share and I cannot shield society from this significant find, even though I do not necessarily agree or understand all of Julian's poignant writings. Like folklore, this story will travel at its own pace.

These words haunt me still to this very day, and I am most fortunate.

1

the day after dying

I opened Julian's manuscript and extracted clarity from a complex set of circumstances. His challenge was to provide society with enough mental flexibility to abandon old belief patterns. Mine is to demonstrate how valuable our choices in life are, and the consequences of those decisions. Julian often wrote and spoke about an enigma called 'G'. When pressed, he would say that G could be applied to anything, and for any purpose, humans wish to create, or destroy.

If I could begin anywhere to reveal the marriage between life and death, identity and fraud, sound mind and delusional episodes, then this is the result. There is no magic in Julian's incarnation; there is just this starting point. The result will be whatever it might be, because the universe does not govern our fate, we do.

Julian wrote the following when he was trapped between an angel and a demon; both of whom he represented whilst preaching on behalf of the Seven Safe Religions.

G IS GONE.

He is no longer. Yesterday killed him, and today I find myself squeezing my hands in prayer with opposing ideals. This anguish I feel inside is written with my blood, and I have you to witness it, should you wish to lend me your third eye.

In a negligent moment, I once asked G who he really was. His reply was swift and disappointing.

'When you know who you are, Julian, then you shall truly recognise me also.' His eyes were ablaze with contempt. Mine were defiant.

The priest in me will tell you with certainty that God will make him accountable for all his tricks. This stranger has complicated my life. Now, after all my efforts in saving souls by giving them a vision of Hell, it is I that needs a lifeline. No longer do I see things through my eyes; I see them through the eyes of the wounded.

Everything I once saw distinctly, is now distorted. The people I touched to heal, suddenly bring me pain. It feels like a curse, this thing G has implanted in my faith. I am beginning to lose passion for my divine calling. The homeless man carries an immortal disease.

During evenings of restlessness, I would visit G down by the breaking surf. My intelligence was threatened when I spoke with this no-name. And my reaction to this was resorting to scripture, instead of conversation. The tide is definitely turning and I'm unsure how low or high it will reach.

Today, in a wave of emotional isolation, I caught sight of G's weather-beaten face in the clouds by the angry sea. My lips formed a halo shape when I realised the depth of my prejudice. I dropped to my knees and sank deep into the sand. I saw how I would strengthen my weaknesses by mocking his wisdom. G only peered at the world through fractured lenses and I was constantly trying to knock them off his face. He needed me, I trained my ego to believe.

I recorded most of our conversations so I could calculate the next tactic. My mission was to convince G to get off the streets and join hands in prayer, and church. The following recording still makes me feel uneasy, and strangely privileged.

'When a person is irrational, then that one has nothing to lose. I envy those who have lost their mind. They don't need the responsibility of thinking for themselves. I envy you for that very reason, Julian.'

I need to get back to work. I have a wife and child to support and I do not want to disappoint them. This entry may be the beginning of nothing.

2

letting go

Being female, I can identify with hormonal changes and the psychological challenges most women deal with every month. To see Julian take this concept a step further in his notes suggested some form of acceptance was taking shape.

'Changes occur naturally on our planet. The twenty-eight days of the moon affects tides, just as a menstrual cycle affects women. Gravity affects the moon and its phase in relation to the sun. People have waxing and waning periods during relationships, and other learning episodes. Orbits affect us all, and we are never out of the loop of life. Even when there is no moonlight on a cold night, the tide moves and keeps life under the surface flowing.' - Julian.

Julian was stepping into a deeper awareness, and G emerged from the grave once more.

I wait for an opportunity to express grief, an emotion that normally bypasses me due to a hardening within. After all, my calling is to comfort others and not be stricken with the same limitations. I feel a silent loneliness creeping in without G whilst trying to stay composed.

My black, hooded jacket keeps me warm on the skin's surface during evenings of preaching. I hunt down contaminated souls and bring them closer to God's expectations. In these dormant hours, the homeless have no chance of avoiding me. Internally, I am shivering and mourn for my lost, delusional friend.

G was one of these lost souls; however, I received more than I signed up for the night we met. His deep-set, shiny, black eyes belonged to a child's nightmare. From his bunker on the beach, his body shifted uncomfortably for a time, until he spoke. Our first words held little respect, but his last words that evening hung like a noose around my neck. He knew I would come back choking on rational thought.

That evening marked the first of many sessions I would spend listening and debating this homeless person's perception of life. He explained how he stepped out of society and found fulfilment on the streets, awakening a broader awareness. G did not want to hear; he only wanted to be heard. I too was doing the same thing. In a sense, he had a job not unlike mine, except he was unpaid and his recruitment prospects were limited.

Night after night I came to find him on the shifting sands. He had a name, a real name given to him at birth, but I did not know it. 'G,' he said.

'G,' I question now, 'what will become of me?'

There is another personality in my life that is a source of contention. I cannot pronounce her name without feeling like all the moisture has drained from my mouth. Her name is highly praised in religious tradition, which only fuelled my obsession. My wife, Mary, and I believed we were blessed to find one another. We secured our standing with the Creator and became parents soon after. Jacqueline is now four years old and shows enthusiasm in religious material.

There is a picture, just one, which I keep with me at all times. I cannot study it without emotion, therefore I have it folded. It belongs in the circle we created where all things sacred are kept. All these items connect with each other in our safe world. There are cracks forming, though. I am doing my best to mend them with my extensive knowledge and training; with hope, commitment, and prayers. Sometimes the cross hanging from my neck is placed in my pocket with them. The cross always lands upside-down, because it is top-heavy without a solid foundation. I carry it regardless. It belongs in my perfect little lie.

There is a perfume that makes my head feel light and my face go askew. Mary hasn't changed her scent since I purchased the first drop. Lately it irritates my nostrils.

I work evenings and am accustomed to waking up in the late afternoon with a ghost lying next to me. Mary prepares me for the night shift ahead with a variety of food packed meticulously in my satchel. The sun is almost setting when I rise like a ravenous wolf. Following our prayers and routine embrace, I bolt out of my life and fill my lungs with what might come.

I am beginning to feel that Mary is no longer mine. At times I consider that she has never belonged to her deeper self either, which is also a defect within me. Her inner workings only recognise the things spoken about in our religion's Safety Literature and its study material. She does not cross that line into territories that belong to those outside the teachings of the Seven Safe Religions. We are immersed together in this Truth, and somehow I have forgotten how to swim for pleasure because all this talk of spiritual survival is weighing me down.

G once highlighted how memories can become more real and meaningful than the present. They are capsules to swallow when you begin to lose feelings of fulfilment. Memories of earlier days with Mary are now becoming more real to me than the humdrum of our daily routine. The predictability in our lives, and the safety net in our existence, have become numbing. I need to experience pain to remind myself that I actually exist. I need to feel the joy in others because I don't think I was born with that gene.

She is Mary, and I no longer feel I am her Julian.

If I could speak; if only I could express my honesty; if only Mary could stop studying the Truth and listen; if only she dared to step out of her isolation and join me in mine, I could reprogram her and allow intruders to set us both free. My wife needs me for the wrong reasons. This is about her now, not me. I am trapped. Mary has become a vision of ash, rather than one of substance and fuel. She is consistently too self-absorbed in her prayers to notice the pain in my eyes or feel my heart skipping to a different beat.

Of late I have found God in the most unlikely places, and Mary will never believe it. She never did believe in me. I only serve as her validation of something else that is all but an illusion created by our insecurities. I was never her righteous knight in shining armour and she was never my Queen; only a distraction, an easy way out of personal growth and self-responsibility. We are a disease handed down by generations of frightened souls too afraid to challenge our better judgement.

3

internal struggle

It has been a considerable length of time between Julian's last entry and the one following. Many new beginnings have since been planted and destroyed. This season of growth was within Julian's reach. He dug deep into the core of human values and removed the stigma of flesh associated with it.

Last night I put to flame twelve candles in order to burn the images of all the apostles. G told me to light my own path so I could construct a legacy unique to myself. It did not go too well. A few things were lost in the fire.

A part of me is dying and needs assistance. I desperately searched the closet, but could not find bootlaces strong enough to hold my bodyweight. It must be God's way of guaranteeing me a slow death, or perhaps, a short-lived recovery. I'm unsure which.

In the mirror I recognise a figure with a scruffy face and unkempt hair. This mirror-man should be balding by now; this reflection should be as grey as a winter storm with lines showing a troubled past, but it looks unaffected by time. My two-dimensional companion reminds me that external appearances do not matter, for they only serve other people.

Internally, I ache as I drag this world along the universe with my nerve endings. My mind is sharp and pointing to the edge of collapse. I struggle to meet my eyes this time for fear of recapturing my previous life and losing sight of my future.

Did I mention my earthly given names were Julian Aquinas Marcus? I no longer exist in the ways your world dictates. I have abandoned my responsibilities bit by bit in order to seek clarity from another source. These things I speak of are involuntarily at times, and I do believe a greater civilisation exists inside my cerebral cortex. My left brain and right brain are no longer married and they share custody of me.

Who said anything about abandonment issues? We all have a disconnect. When was the last time you revisited the womb of reality? We all have the same genetic illness, and infinite potential. So, which parent do you favour; the one on your right, the one on your left, or the one you adopt?

When I was a very young and lonely child, signs of God were all around me. I heard His voice respond to questions I never knew I wanted answered. I saw Him in shapes and angels when they appeared in my room late at night. These helpers would take my hand and lead me to another world where everyone gave me attention. I thought God was showing me the path to a happy life whilst I used my Earth body, but then things got out of control. The older I got, the more sorrow I felt inside. It seemed like nobody understood or cared about me or my experiences. I was tormented and popular at the same time. Everyone likes a freak show for different reasons. Although loved by my family, it was never enough to pull me through my depression. The longer I stayed with them, the more homesick I became for my secret family. At nine, I desperately waited for some kind of signal.

The first rays of sunlight filtered into my bedroom and a pattern formed on my beige walls that could be described as prison-cell issue. Configurations of gold and black lines crept across my face, and the intensity licked my eyes into a state of awareness. I momentarily regained lost enthusiasm.

Foremost on my mind was 'Flicker', our new television set. Flicker was made available by some kind of immaculate conception, because it was too expensive in our household and came from mysterious means.

The early hours of sun-up gave me ample opportunity to master the art of flicking whilst my big brother slept heavily. Early morning cartoons usually rewarded me, but even they slept at this hour. Test-screens on the first four flicks proved disappointing. The next one crushed my aspiration.

'Politics? Who watches politics this early in the morning?' I questioned in a house full of sleepers.

Another push revealed a sixth channel that was too snowy to watch. That was it, the whole pathetic selection. Undeterred, I continued to force down each plastic square – over and over again I thumb-surfed with the persistence only a child could achieve without developing some form of repetitive stress disorder. Then the inevitable battery failure put a stop to the compulsion.

I thrust the controller at the brown couch. It bounced onto the next seat just as 'Jesus!' came roaring from the television's speaker.

'Jesus?' I echoed suspiciously. I repositioned myself and placed the remote between my knees. 'What do you know about Jesus?'

The man on the tube was youthful looking and wasn't dressed in any of the traditional garb I was accustomed to seeing at church services. This gentleman in Technicolor seemed like a suave superhero to a kid. He wore a white suit and a red tie, and darted around the stage with lots of energy. I searched the set design for traditional church architecture and religious ornaments, but found none.

'That's no church,' I observed. 'Looks like the Opera House, or something?'

Unbeknownst to me, I was actually watching an American Evangelist at work. The illusion of grandeur captivated the heart and soul of paid entertainment whilst the complex, sensitive issues of religion bowled me over once again. I had naively believed for some time that all religions were one book, one cover, and one faith. The planting of a seed to reach God through religion was never rooted deep enough into my being to accept.

The Evangelist blasted his willing congregation with direct and indirect Scriptures from a book that rested precariously on the palm of his hand. A faithful gathering clung to every word, as if Satan was about to challenge their faith. Gone were the traditional droned-out speeches consisting of mind-numbing dialogue; instead, raw emotion bordering on hysterics kept these pews alert.

This explosive episode profoundly affected me – the isolated child and non believer – as I observed the proceedings in a state of ambiguity. I was the unbeliever wanting to believe the unbelievable. The showman captured my arousing curiosity and sense of vulnerability. The idea of self-promoting oneself as God's personal messenger had never entered my mind before. It sounds so egotistical, yet this man spewed forth such authority that I felt compelled to listen to his sermon.

A mass exorcism, executed by a few powerful statements and hand gestures, was in progress. The performance had the full auditorium spellbound to every letter of his interpretation of the law. Free of any inhibitions, they too became part of the act.

I sat on the edge of my seat. Swellings from other personal stings of disappointment had not yet subsided, therefore I cautiously watched with trepidation.

'If you have faith in Jesus Christ, Satan will no longer reside in your sick heart.'

The glass box filled with talk of evil and powers of demonic attachment. Thousands of faithful souls squirmed in the religious frenzy. Hysteria without the rage that frequented my household filled every grainy pixel on the tube. Faith was at stake here, the unconditional kind, and I briefly considered this concept of freedom. I looked for clues in order to give myself permission to continue watching this vociferous man and his claims. Despite the charisma and energy of the preacher, I waited for something more than words to lure me in emotionally.

Eventually, I asked God aloud if I should keep watching this man speak about these things called 'Jesus' and 'Satan'. I asked Flicker the same question. I hesitated for a moment before attempting to remove the image with a finger movement on the controller. The man did not leave my lounge room. So I hit the controller firmly to wake it up.

'Come on, change!' I pleaded, despite my answer being revealed. The option of manually changing the station on the television box was cheating, so I gave it one last long, hard press. 'Come on!' It was no use. Flicker was drained of life in desperate hands. 'What the?'

In a moment of significance, God's spokesperson captured my full attention. Unnervingly, the preacher turned to me, the unbeliever, and focused on my dejected soul. My heart skipped a few beats and shame suddenly appeared in my emotional tree, as if I was caught doing something that defies my good nature. My eyes fell into the man's deeply troubling awareness of my sins. A mutual telepathy took place followed by critical words that helped deliver a response. As with any perfect sales pitch, the fear of missing out always overrides logic – especially when a life-changing opportunity presents itself and comes with no obvious cost. A gift was on offer in the form of unconditional acceptance of the suit, God, or was it Jesus? Being 'saved', which was an entirely new concept for me, was now foremost on my mind, regardless of who did the operation.

'If you are hurting with any kind of pain, simply put your hand on your television screen and have faith in Jesus Christ.' The voice spoke to me directly from a place of knowing. 'Together we can expel those hurtful things from your body and from your mind.'

Submissively, I allowed the penetration of an American prophet to examine my forgotten soul and invert me. I revealed all my shortcomings to the God federation through this two way mirror. The chant-like manner of the blessed painted confusion and hope. The ailing and spiritually weak were helped onto the stage by assistants. Some were wheelchair-bound, whilst others simply zombie-dead inside.

'No way?' I mouthed.

The white suit then declared that he was going to perform a miracle through his faith in Jesus Christ. I fostered this concept and added it to the 'Wow!' experiences in my life thus far. There was a catch to being saved. The need to believe in the power of Christ, whom I knew nothing about, was the skeleton key to sanity.

To assist viewers at home, the producers had created a simple, white, paper cut-out hand and placed it in front of the camera. With this modern technology, the process of healing was made available to anyone with an antenna. Without recollection of how I got there, I sat close to the television screen and placed my sticky hand on the image, waiting for further instructions. I could hear the static electricity popping between this world and the new one buzzing around my hair.

I had to prove to my God, Jesus, and the white suit that I was willing to fix all which must surely be broken in my young body. I vowed to no longer write-off the dusty pages of the Bible as a mere fairytale for tradition's sake. I was on the verge of clearing all my heartache. I needed to believe that ridding my soul of the invisible beast, which had apparently been deceiving me all along, would fix my childhood problems.

Staying focused as a kid could possibly tolerate, I sat determined. This new five-minute faith had to be realised or I might forever lose another opportunity to be free of burdens.

After I pushed through another four-second concentration span, I felt an energy shift and it allowed room for more open-mindedness. Desperately maintaining my stance in an uncomfortable physical position, I tenaciously pressed harder against the idiot box. My small hand was engulfed by the cheap, paper hand image. The Holy Spirit appeared to be working alongside the gremlins to make my experience fully realised. The dynamic preacher consistently examined the student for weaknesses and kept on grilling me.

'Hold nothing back! Concentrate!' the Evangelist screamed. 'You MUST have more faith!'

In the minutes that followed, an unbearable strain caused veins to pop out from my smooth golden skin. Droplets of faith baptised the carpet, and I was on the verge of cracking from this spiritual punishment. Hysteria in the congregation had reached fever pitch and the final act was in process. The paper hand was removed from time to time so I could be with the worshippers and bathe in their glory.

'Through Jesus Christ you are cured!'

I watched incomprehensibly as each God-fearing Christian fell to earth, overwhelmed by the power of Christ no doubt, while the cleansed brothers and sisters swiftly caught them. All this pandemonium was set amongst a backdrop of worshippers singing songs of praise with hands in the air. One by one, the ailing rose to their feet and confessed all their illnesses were removed. They praised Jesus and were taken off stage whilst maintaining their euphoric state.

The unlikely Messiah abruptly stopped his insane onslaught and declared victory over the deceiver of all men. He then looked directly at me as I reached breaking point in my stance and concentration.

'You, the one I am saving, through the love of Jesus, you are cured!'

I slid my hand off the television screen and fell in a heap on the floor. I tried to regain muscle memory. It was early morning and I was exhausted. I sat up and took a deep breath. I gave the light an opportunity to enter me. I exhaled deeply to push evil darkness out, and… NOTHING!

Nothing had shifted. I was the same me in the same house in the same life. Nothing happened. I was expecting a metamorphosis to take place, where I would emerge as a new being drained of bad blood. I wanted to be carried away into a Utopian landscape that I had often dreamt about. Anything, except this.

My heavy heart strained further under the Lord's disapproval. It seemed that I was forever unworthy of a church-God's love. Dark thoughts entered my imagination with lightning speed.

A stark realisation sprung forth. 'Maybe I was born doomed? I focussed back on the tube.

The credits were rolling. Something about donating money and valuables so the good work could continue and more people be saved.

I stood and dived on the controller near the couch. I pointed it towards the box, and fired the 'off' button. There was an instant silence, but the white noise in my head continued to distract me for some time.

4

beyond context

I found side notes within some of Julian's work. He revealed how he suffered from 'Bleedthrough', which he described as an automatic writing, trance-like state. These scratches of the imagination will become transparent as we delve deeper into his complex mind. Julian would use pencil and paper to write almost superhuman-like without analysing what was being written, or who was using his hand to write it.

I posed many questions to Julian over the years whilst forming a career at Cathedral Psychiatric Clinic. I recall watching him drink black coffee from a mug when his overgrown, messy hair took a dip. He pulled his fringe to the side with his fingertips and squeezed the moisture onto the cafe floor. Customers noticed his behaviour, but he either wasn't aware of them or didn't care. This seemed like the perfect opportunity to ask him a philosophical question to see how he really measured up to my expectations of a mentor.

'What is the human's best quality?'

His reply was swift and not some Texas Hold'em delay. Julian seemed to step out as someone else stepped in. His childlike mannerisms went missing for a moment. A tone of authority reached out to me across the table. An all encompassing confidence appeared. It felt otherworldly. His tone had a believable edge of mystery and I was frightened and excited at the same time.

'Shadows,' a voice replied from the ether. 'They are perfect because they cause no harm, even when people who cast them do harm. There is no blood lost, no pain felt, no tree uprooted, no heart broken, and no clearer image to measure the human's psyche from a safe dimension.'

This outer-inner body experience was something I would witness repeatedly in our time thereafter. As a trained therapist, it was difficult for me not to over-analyse this phenomenon. As a friend, I could easily accept Julian with all his quirky personality traits.

Julian's eyes dropped towards my spicy chai latte, as if nothing extraordinary took place, and asked me if I was dairy intolerant.

'Yes, Julian,' I replied. 'Yes, I am.'

I'm ashamed to acknowledge it and yet I'll reveal it anyhow. Lately, it seems, I have incarnated into some kind of mind specialist. There is nothing special about any profession so do not make a fuss over mine. You are special, my dearest patient, and my most trusted psychoanalyst. We will play doctor together and will forget which of us needs assistance. I won't remind you that you're ill, or that I have somehow managed to get inside of you to escape me.

I have tasted your bitter-sweet love and felt the effects of the withdrawal. When history catches up with tomorrow, the frightened lambs will challenge the wolves and artificial faiths will vanish from our realities. Until then, walk with your own shadow because that is your true shape.

I remind my human how ugly he is at times whenever I catch a reflective surface. When I dim the lights, I see an outline of a figure with unmatched potential. Details can be hideous, but imagination can create an abundance of beauty. There is always hope in bleak times.

Everything in life is terminal, and somehow I see death breathing life into existence. Death is a blessing, not a curse. Modern religions will tell you different, of course they will. Still, death can cripple the human spirit when we lose someone close to us. It is a heartfelt loss, not a revenge killing by God. I know what it feels like to lose someone close. I am still searching for every one of you in this carnage I have caused.

We live in a modern society. A sample of your breath will diagnose most physical illnesses, yet it does nothing to reveal your mental state. People tell lies well and can be convincing. Not long ago, it took up to twelve years to determine mental illness. Now it takes one hour with an ear probe, but it seems these modern techniques don't work on me.

Post-traumatic stress disorder has become a pandemic in this new decade, despite relative peace on our planet. The Seven Safe Religions were primarily responsible for this latest rape of consciousness, the aftermath of years of indoctrination. They are no longer in power, as you well know – unless you live in the past or are embroiled in some kind of conspiracy theory. Bad religion lingers in my mind like a permanent lucid dream. It survives in my conscience like cancer and will eventually be the death of me, which will finally free my shadow.

I have achieved great things in a slither of time, the silly ones tell me, but a lifetime can seem like a lifetime when all you want is out. Patients often shower me with kindness after I insult them. People much like you try to get closer whilst I take a few more steps towards the door.

People tell me their problems and some speak highly of me. They say my intellect is great. This is frightening because I seldom know who speaks to them when my lips move. I'm unworthy of their praise; I once crippled those who I now try to mend.

Sometimes I feel as if I'm riding a wave that is going to destroy everything in its path. I'm riding Armageddon, and God has my feet planted on the bomb. I have to remind myself that I did not create the wave. I have to believe that good things come from terrible acts. I can no longer deny my vulnerability. I will crash hard and have no choice but to take others out on my way down. It is not my will to do so; it is of the Father's, is it not? Yes, that is convenient.

5

psychiatry is an addiction

Julian continued to write in a self-loathing and highly provocative manner, bringing someone else's voice onto the page. This short entry is when Julian's 'Bleedthrough' accounts with an entity, or his undiagnosed mental condition, began to surface. Bleedthrough inserted its psychology of persuasion into my psyche, and was the catalyst for this book, Acupuncture of The Mind.

There is a keyhole of unlimited imagination I simply refer to as the 'the womb'. A jolt of reality usually has a narcotic taste to it whenever I revisit this place of creative being. In your reality I have obstacles and barriers, such as placing conditions on people who place conditions on people. In the womb, I simply create for the sake of my personal growth and exist in self-governing choice. For this reason, please consider destroying all I reveal to you, because under the heat of human conditions, hatred and blame become hot conveniences. I will occasionally speak metaphorically in order to pull you further away from tradition; to exercise your mind; to gravitate you into self-awareness. You too will experience the violation of my imagination and rid the disease of primitive thought.

Although Cathedral Psychiatric Clinic statistically rates top dog when it comes to patient rehabilitation, it's not a fair and complete finding. The quest for implementing impossible cures is a distraction from my own fractures. I heal others to mask my weaknesses. In this process of goodwill, each success story is another scoop of dirt I dig out of the ground for my own burial; sinking me further into a gothic lullaby.

You see, goodwill is actually a selfishness; a search for greater awareness of the self. Can you see what is happening here? Of course not. You're just pretending like all the others do; but stay a little longer and we can figure it out together. The last time I checked you were still in my care.

My head questions my psychiatric abilities and the sorcery of my practices. Schizophrenia comes to mind and so too does possession. The priest in me is always searching for someone else to blame. My personalities are multiplying, and I do not have room for another one, but more are coming. I see them forming when I sleep. I feel them enter you as you hear these words echo in your sticky mind. We are all connected. I want to be nonhuman again so I can understand the human psyche without participating in this gene pool of blood sports. I would also like to share my experiences with you; the ones on the other side, the dead observers.

'Follow nobody and you won't die tainted,' G once told me. That is not easy. Beyond the womb, life has become overcrowded with hurtful experiences. A baby without judgement and clear conscience, I am not.

In the old system, born-again Christians said they found Jesus. Missionaries boasted how they helped tribal communities by spreading the Good News. Cultic movements rewrote the truth daily.

Muslims said there is but one God, Allah, and we must follow His commands. The Roman Catholic Church tried to squeeze old worlds into a new one. Buddha sat happily as Buddhists paid homage to laws of freedom. Pagans worshipped the stars and anything that fitted around their necks, placing God within inanimate objects. Satanists declared Satan to be misunderstood.

It takes years, centuries, for cults to evolve and develop a core belief system. It only takes a second for those religions to split into a thousand new faiths. Literally, let me step aside for a moment and see what God requests me to write down on His behalf, if you are that way inclined.

If you can only find Me in a rulebook, then your book is out of date and certainly not My work.
If you can only appease Me by gathering in large crowds, then you are afraid to be with Me alone.
If your God is a religion, then your faith belongs to man, not in Me.
If you feel the need to sell Me, then you make Me look tacky and overpriced.
If the biblical Jesus is your saviour, then who will save Jesus from your special needs?

I say, never lift my words above your own. My will is mine alone. Do not follow me or anyone else blindly to the ends of the earth, because someone will always push you off. There is a long line of followers and very few independents. Start your own path by clearing the weeds.

it begins with G and ends with Bliss

Despite his best efforts, Julian had little chance of destroying old memories. He stepped in and out of portals, from one experience to the next and back again. Some were uncomfortable admissions that needed to be owned. Others were pools of illuminating potential. Every day at the clinic was a challenge and blessing for me. I tried rationalising his frequency of communication and often received mixed messages. Psychiatry Professors often teach that it's a straightforward science figuring out who, and to what degree, someone is affected by the 300 or so classifications of mental conditions. Julian has shown me first hand that mental health is a subjective and complex world not to be categorised by causes and effects.

During my evenings with G, my ego became a higher priority than goodwill. I blinked and somehow avoided what came next. It took me years to catch up to a distant star, which would guide me through the worst of what I created. There is no logic behind certain laws, therefore my ego kept my faith alive.

The final whispers of the dying man were written in a loud voice for the sole purpose of converting me from a life of unchallenging clichés to one of independence and growth. The vagrant showed me his palace and highlighted how it was I who lived in squalor, in demographic filth.

I deceived myself by thinking how my life consisted of culture and awesome authority. The sidewalk scholar touched my sense of sensibility. Now I move forward by recalling and recording experiences honestly in the hope that the impossible nature of my truth will sit right with those on my critical list. My own name is always at the top of that crisis file.

There is a clinical condition known as 'temporary insanity'. Everyone's life is temporary and to think otherwise is insane. The hope of Armageddon to be upon us so we, the chosen, don't taste death is ignorant and selfish. To fear the unknown of death is temporary insanity until your own death departs you from this state called human existence.

Before I began this search for balance, when I was merely a child learning to walk, I already understood many theories on the subject of fantasy reality. An imaginary friend named Kafka was with me during my formative years. Practicality is hidden from children just as innocence is hidden from adults. Over the leap years I had learned to suppress certain experiences because my parents inserted a colour chart into my life. It only contained two shades: black and white.

Many lost ideals will eventually find their way into a collective consciousness. Works of fiction and nonfiction are both touched by a colourful imagination, always written by man, woman, or child, and eventually destroyed by education or boredom.

A psychiatrist bears the brunt of many obstacles, and the grip on sanity is often bleached with inexplicable personal dealings not taught by university lecturers. Logic is never clear-cut because everyone has a different view of reason. Exercising the mind leads to all kinds of complications. A jogger goes nowhere fast when using the convenience of a treadmill, but the body still feels the jolts. The Earth stopped moving, and I hit my head hard on the surface of madness. The tug-of-war between imagination and actuality is challenging, even for the unchallenged.

Ever since my disassociation with the Seven Safe Religions, my wife and I fell into marital problems. Separation was inevitable. An enormous pressure comes about when one renounces faith in government and/or religious ties whilst the other clings unreservedly. New laws automatically divorce couples after two years of separation, which is helpful for procrastinating spouses.

Mary, like so many others, struggled with the new freedoms of a modern world. She was taught to follow and is incapable of leading her own life based on autonomy. Despite my inside knowledge, I was powerless to influence Mary in another direction away from the rotten harvest. Love, or convenient partnerships, can often be a hindrance in certain situations.

The person I once was is a fraud. My entire being was wrapped tight in an invisible sheath whilst observing my surroundings with limited movement, restricting the brain from breathing. My personal relationship with the self was being compromised in my former life, and I encouraged the abuse. Religion can often mimic a marriage with its expectations and sole devotion. Eventually, I remembered where home really was: always on the other side of the door through which I entered this world.

From my emotional ledge, I see Mary looking up towards me, throwing her arms to the sky and surrendering to needs of the church. She has free will, I know this, but I also see her in bondage. I believe religious people are defective because they keep putting their soul in a poker machine called Blind Faith.

I have poison on my tongue, I know. Does my internal conflict stem from bitterness, empathy, loneliness, frustration, insanity, revenge, honesty, or something much more complicated and unforgiving? I sense my transparency will become painfully evident in these pages.

There is a new woman in my life. This person is not a face beneath the sheets when I desire release; however, she creates tension by offering friendship on my heaviest days. I often struggle with her clinical conduct and schoolgirl sophistication. Bliss Stone is an intern. Technically, I am her boss. Like most men in the company of young beauty, I have weaknesses. Fortunately, my respect for Bliss is greater than my mortal needs, and this keeps my hands in my pockets and my head in my occupation. The 'higher cause clause' could actually be the excuse I need to hide my sexual inferiority complex.

It's time to dive into the depths and expose the things ripping me apart during turbulent evenings. There is forever a prophecy to fulfil and I have no marketing plan. I do however see an arrangement to teach you something I quite simply know nothing about.

dim light

On my first day at Cathedral I had reservations about Julian and his professionalism. He was awkward, like a child stuck in a man's body. He struck me as someone who did not care about his appearance or manner within a professional environment. He was supposed to be someone who could propel my career in psychology and beyond. I was seeking a mentor and all I saw was a man beaten by life and carrying the eyes of the wounded. He was dragging his feet like somebody was holding him by the ankles.

I came prepared, so I thought, and had to be open-minded with warranted concern. After all, this was a psychiatrist with a chequered reputation. The only thing he conformed to was being a nonconformist. My first impressions were confusing to say the least. This person, it seemed to me, was incapable of holding his own mind still, so how was he expected to enter someone else's and bring them forth to a place of reason?

From rusty sheets of iron, magnificent structures are built. I was so busy analysing Julian in those first few minutes that I failed to understand the strength of his framework. Then, he centred my attention by answering a question with the capacity of either a highly evolved individual or someone on the other end of the scale; a confused primate.

The question itself was immaterial, because it was dwarfed by a philosophical response.

'Life stops when we are balanced,' he said. 'There's no opposing forces motivating us to suck in another breath and move us forward.'

The opposite of our perception of reality is often true, I would learn quickly. After a few sittings, I was lured by romantic adversity to step out of my comfort zone and walk the halls of Cathedral with my new mentor. It was never going to be a straightforward journey, and my father, a highly respected criminal psychiatrist, tried to stop me from taking that blind corner.

Julian reached for his pencil and large hardcover journal – my original copy of his authorship – and wrote the following passages of insight.

Underneath my skin is the number of the beast. I am that number, and the Seven Safe Religions was the beast that kept me on its radar by inserting it there. The former things have passed away, and humans are no longer rounded up for updating personal data. I choose not to have my splinter removed. I consented to this violation, and the small scar upon removal would only serve to remind me of my hypocrisy. Although responsibility can be burdensome, it can also be liberating at times.

Those who feel they don't belong in our society have real reasons to seek solitude. They say, 'Feel my mysterious skin and then tell me we are not of the same flesh.' We are intolerant of these street creatures. We distrust them and are afraid of our cousins. I understood long ago that black holes in the universe are occurring in suburban streets and we create the suction by pulling at the plug of responsibility. My mysterious skin proves that I too remain part of the problem.

In my late teens I had a few months to think about my future prospects regarding a career. My parents did not pay good money for me to attend a religious boarding school only to spend my days playing computer games in my flat. Although they were neither highly religious, nor moved in political circles, they had opportunistic traits. It frustrated them to see me sit in neutral whilst the world around me was changing. Their expectations of me consisted of the very things they were not; career driven. So we decided I should go to The Eleventh Hour Theological Seminary.

There are many grizzly bits of information to chew before committing to a life of worship. Whether to swallow or spit out undigested remains was always a struggle for me in my youth, yet I swallowed most of the time. As a teenager in boarding school, I acted like a bulimic regurgitating spiritual food behind closed doors. I was convinced all this nourishment was making me ill. With a bitter tongue, I would pray against the very thing I was becoming, a convert.

I wasn't looking for signs to point me in the right direction anymore, they just seemed to appear at random intersections. The following experience occurred when I was contemplating my future as a servant of the Seven Safe Religions. It propelled me to do humanitarian work under the 'Truth' program, and I enrolled in a counselling course within their organisation. At the time, it seemed like a rational option full of promise. I thought it was a signal from God. Maybe it was.

Manna was falling from the sky in mid winter when I cooked up a storm in my one bedroom villa – spicy chicken at its best. Exotic Indian aromas and thick flavours still line my tastebuds when I recall the meal. The evening in question also carried a warming blanket of strangeness, as I sat alone on my couch waiting for something to happen.

With half my meal digesting and the other half still on the bench, I contemplated another evening of online videos followed by heavy reading. This ritual was a precedent for restless sleep. Even though I chose to live on my own, I loathed being alone all the same. I did have a girlfriend at the time, yes, Mary, but we resisted temptation.

A faint tapping at my door peeled me away from the sofa with slight annoyance. I loved documentaries. I pulled back the blinds and hit the light switch. My dimly lit porch revealed a face in the gloom. A man I didn't recognise faced me.

'Can I help you?' I asked. The gentleman stood silent for some time. He looked stunned, like roadkill seconds before death. The stranger wore jeans and a thin V-neck jumper. That was it; nothing on his grubby feet or beneath his sweater. Despite being unshaven, he did not look overly derelict or menacing. His lightly peppered hair was trimmed at a respectable length. I estimated this fellow to be in his late thirties. His most striking feature was his innocent blue eyes that appeared friendly and innocent.

'Can you help me?' he asked. His tone was awash with uncertainty and hurt.

'If I can,' I replied. 'Has your car broken down?' He looked at me blankly.

'I don't drive.'

'Do you need a lift home?'

'No. I'm looking for my parents,' he said. 'I don't want to go home.'

The confusion began.

'I'm Julian.' I extended my arm to shake his hand. He responded by tilting his head up and offering me a shy, warm smile.

'I'm Paul.'

'Hi Paul, do you know your parents' address or phone number?'

'No. Could you look it up for me, please? They live in this area.'

An aura of body odour surrounded Paul's otherwise pleasant persona. I momentarily contemplated an invitation inside, but the action was promptly suppressed by the prospect of trying to eradicate his smell from my lounge. Besides, I had comfortable chairs on my small veranda we could utilise.

Seconds later I took a few steps away from Paul to get my phone. When I returned I asked him about his parents.

'They live near those big lights and a river,' he explained, as if he was there recently.

'The Stadium?' I understood. 'What name should I look up?'

'My last name's Carmichael.' He then spelt it out letter by letter.

'Sorry, Paul, there's no one with that name publicly listed in that area,' I explained. His chest sank a little, and I told him I'd check another website just to make sure.

'Thank you,' he said.

'I'll be back in a minute. I'm going to put the jug on, would you like a cup of tea or coffee?'

'Yes, please. Coffee, please… I have four teaspoons of sugar and milk.'

'Okay, Paul, I'll just do a quick search while the jug's on the boil,' I said. 'Just relax and make yourself comfortable.'

The other website did not tell me anything more than I already knew. The name Carmichael or any other variant of the name was not listed in that immediate vicinity.

I returned outside with the hot drinks and then sat with him before explaining the situation. He thanked me for the coffee and every other insignificant act. The evening air bit through my clothing, and my eyes fell to Paul's bare feet. He must have been walking without shoes since he was an infant. The outer edges of his soles looked leathery and cracked. The flesh underneath his feet were as tough as my hiking boots, I imagined.

'Paul,' I began gently, 'my father is a diabetic who needs medication for survival. Are you on any medication?'

'No.' He seemed confident in his response.

'Is there anyone else I can call for you?'

'I have a brother here somewhere, but I don't know where he lives.' He shrugged and looked towards the property entrance.

'Have you ever been to his place?'

'No, he moved.' Paul silently reflected great loss. His coffee mug was empty, and I offered a refill.

I returned to the kitchen and boiled the jug again, but I knew it would not nourish him. I placed leftover spicy chicken and rice into my microwave and poured boiling water into his cup. Upon handing my guest the food, Paul's face glowed with appreciation. Patiently, I eased into my deckchair and began to unravel the mystery of his visit. Eventually I would become privy as to how he ended up on my doorstep on that auspicious evening, and still it would appear senseless.

I lived in the second unit in a row of five. A huge timber fence concealed the property, and the only access was a dark driveway that ran parallel to the row of flats. There were many other dwellings more accessible and visible along the streetscape, and I was curious why Paul ended up on my unlit porch. The fourth unit down had a low voltage globe glowing in the darkness and would have seemed a more logical choice to seek assistance.

'Paul, are you from around here?' I asked. 'Where's your home, exactly?'

His body sank deeper into the padded chair. I felt he would tell me anything I asked as long as my questions were specific.

'I came from Dustmore,' he said.

'Dustmore? Is that where your home is?' I asked for clarification.

Paul looked temporarily confused before placing his thoughts together.

'I grew up in Dustmore and lived there with my parents, and my brother.'

'And then you all moved to the Coast?' I asked.

'No,' he replied.

'Okay, so what happened?'

'First my brother moved out of home, then my parents moved to be around him.'

'What about you?' I questioned. 'Where did you go?'

'I stayed around home.'

Something inside me shifted uncomfortably. Feelings of abandonment still troubled me.

'When was the last time you saw your parents?' I asked.

'Lots of years.'

'Paul, you know they could have moved elsewhere.'

'Yes,' he sighed.

'When did you arrive here on the Coast this time around?'

'A week ago.'

'How did you get all the way here from Dustmore?'

'I walked,' he simply stated.

'You walked?' I raised my eyebrows in amazement. I had looked up Dustmore as we spoke. 'You know it takes about eight hours by car to get to Dustmore, don't you?'

'No, I didn't.'

Paul finished his meal along with his second cup of coffee. I offered him another drink, which he kindly accepted.

'How did you end up here, with me now?'

'I don't know.' He seemed troubled by the question's complexity.

'Did you forget?'

'I mean, I don't know why. I know how I did it,' he tried to clarify. 'I was walking next to a road and someone in a car stopped next to me. They said they will drive me.'

'Where were they taking you?'

'They didn't tell me, but I told them I wanted to go to my parents place near the river and big lights.'

'But this road leads to a dead end. The location you want is on the other side and much further away. So why did you end up here exactly?'

'The man in the car dropped me off in your street. I walked, and then I stopped in the driveway, and then walked to your door. I knocked on your door. My brain said knock on this door.'

Despite the situation, it did not feel creepy at all.

'Well, I am glad you did, Paul.'

I was convinced that Paul would be generous to others if he had the opportunity to do so.

'Could you take me to the hospital?' he requested unexpectedly. 'They'll know what to do with me there.'

'The hospital? Have you been to the public hospital before?'

'Yes, I sometimes go there at night,' Paul admitted.

'As a patient?'

'No, to get warm and sometimes people give me food. They'll know what to do with me,' he repeated. 'It's the best place for me to go now.'

'What about a homeless shelter?'

'I tried once, but they don't have room.' Paul's eyes began to develop a layer of thick moisture. It might have been the result of exhaustion or sorrow. 'Thank you for helping me.'

My feeble attempts to help him were no match for his situation. I made a few enquiries on his behalf, yet failed to find a bed for the night at any refuge centre.

'Do you have any belongings?' I asked, despite guessing the obvious.

'I have my clothes. I did have a watch, but not anymore.'

'You must be freezing. I'm wearing more clothes than you and I'm shivering!'

'I get cold, but I'm not cold now,' he replied.

'If you want me to take you to the hospital, I will, but I don't think they can help you much there. Before we go anywhere, I'll just go inside and get a few things. I'll be back in a minute.'

'I'll just sit here. Is that alright?'

'Of course it is. I won't be long.'

I struggled to come to terms with this poor fellow sleeping out in the cold. Without hesitation, I pulled a big sports bag out of a cupboard and, on passing the recliner, tore the blue cotton blanket from it. Reaching down, I grabbed my new joggers from the floor and two pairs of socks from the clean laundry basket. From the refrigerator I collected a carton of juice. In the pantry I found a few savoury items, and on the kitchen bench, bananas and apples were tossed in as well.

Paul remained quiet when I returned outside with the temporary basic survival pack. I handed it to him and explained that it was the best I could do. My eyes probably told a different story. It wasn't the best at all, but still, I believed it was adequate. He thanked me again, and I asked him to put the shoes on for size, which were obviously too big.

'You're swimming in them!' I joked. To my pleasure he let a little laugh slip out. In that instant I saw more human being than my eyes, ears, and nostrils had allowed me to acknowledge earlier. He paced the length of my small veranda in his clown shoes, thanking me often. I offered him another hot drink before we were due to depart and he declined it. I marvelled at how he didn't ask to use the bathroom after all those liquids.

'Julian, instead of driving me to the hospital, could you just call the police and they will pick me up from here? I don't want to bother you anymore.'

Was he playing on my emotions? He appeared completely genuine in that moment of diminishing options. He didn't wish anyone to fuss over him and never pleaded for charity. Not from me at least.

'Are you sure you want me to do that?'

'Yes please.' Paul was certain the police department would take care of him. A night in the lockup was now foremost in his mind.

'Okay, if that's what you really want I'll make the call.'

In the following hour I sat with Paul on my dimly lit porch and we spoke few words, although it was not boring. He was like an old friend who had come to visit after a long absence, and I could sense he felt comfortable with me. The drifter was obviously tired and he allowed himself to zone out on his chair whilst clutching onto another warm mug, as if embracing embers of a glowing, cherished memory.

Finally a police wagon pulled into the driveway. Two officers emerged from the blinding lights pointing directly at us. I don't know what the x-ray revealed when we shielded our eyes. I handed Paul the bag along with some coins. His face sunk with despair. I heard the air rush out of his lungs. Not even the noise of the police truck idling could muffle such heartache. Softly, he thanked me for the last time.

'You again!' an officer roared. 'This is the third time this week! I told you last time, there is nothing we can do for you!'

'Is everything all right, anything I can do?' I inquired, regretting the situation I had created.

'We'll deal with it,' he replied bluntly. 'We have better things to do than be a taxi service!' The law continued to use heavy words on Paul, and I was powerless to lighten them.

In hindsight, their reaction seemed reasonable. They had serious crimes to attend to and were more than likely understaffed. An officer placed Paul in the back of the truck – the same space that held criminals of all descriptions. After all, he was a crim in the eyes of the law, because he had no fixed address.

Paul was told he would be dropped off at the shelter, even though he would be turned away by the staff there. The police also informed him that he would have to sort himself out because there were simply not enough services available. The vehicle rolled away and I felt miserable. Paul the criminal; public enemy number one; the most unwanted. How distorted. How wrong.

My brief encounter with Paul did not reveal a man capable of doing harm or a person addicted to substances. Some would argue such a person should be medicated – why? How is being on mind altering meds going to make a bed available at a homeless shelter, nourish a hungry body, or generate respect?

My shower was warm that night, my bed even warmer, yet my faith in the system was as cold as the dark side of the moon, which is always hidden from our view.

A couple of years later I began my humanitarian occupation. Hired by the Seven Safe Religions, I walked the boulevards, parks and beaches with the firm belief that my efforts were making a contribution to society, and God's chosen people.

A drop of red wine no longer befriends any faith; it simply stains my memory. I forgot where my mouth was when I became a puppet for organised religions. There is nothing left to say about my homeless friend, Paul. For it has all been said before, and we will forever pretend we did not hear a word of it.

diving into a tunnel

How does one explain the following without getting caught up in fluffy nonsense? Whilst Julian recalls this incident from an emotional point of view, I will retrieve the line he used on that very day.

'Balance is for those blinded by life, not guided by it.'

Unstable clients stretch out on my couch one after another like fallen angels. Many patients come to me after making no progress with other traditionally experienced therapists, much to the dislike of those experts.

My procedures are unorthodox, raw, and uninhibited. They often lack obvious direction. I don't have a name for my style of therapy, but one might consider it to be a blend of Quantum Psychology and a funeral party. I experience the realm of disturbances along with my patients and nail myself in the coffin with them. Once inside, I try to locate life in the emptiness of sorrow, shock, or hurt. When I find it, I defend both of us against a veil of illusions. Most of the time the emotionally battered individuals fight with me. I have also emerged from the coffin alone numerous times.

Periodically, my patients overwhelm me with their pain. Sometimes, my job description is lost along with my identity, as empathy overrides clinical behaviour. This happened yesterday. I record it today because I've had time to empty my glasses of whisky, allowing the spirit to filter through. I'm sober now and ready to reveal to you what Rosemary Anne Smith has taught me.

'Jacob likes comic books,' she said.

'Squeeze my finger, Rosemary.'

'Jacob likes comic books,' she repeated without following my request.

Rosemary was flat on her back, unresponsive. Her heavily dyed, black hair strewn across crispy, white hospital linen. Her face was pale and without makeup. Rosemary's eyes remained open, distant and pink-raw.

Earlier, I had gently removed the tape from her eyelids that kept them permanently closed. I placed drops of lubricant on her eyes. She was fixated on something within. She did not even flinch when the droplets pounded her, or when my searchlight rummaged through her optic sensors. Rosemary had been this way for a few days. Her diagnostic tests revealed nothing abnormal on a physical level.

My patient is the sole survivor of a bombing that took place during a small church service. It was the result of a custody dispute involving one of the other patrons. We have no proof of who Jacob is, although one might guess from all accounts that Rosemary is referring to her son. Public records indicate the boy's real name was Jamison; however, we have been informed that in recent times Rosemary began calling him Jacob because of her religiosity. Tragically, her son lost his life in a drowning accident a year earlier.

In this hospital across town, Rosemary was fed intravenously and strapped to a bed for her own safety, despite lying still as a corpse. In my possession I had a box full of her personal effects, including photographs, home movies, music, clothing, and her ex-husband's aftershave. I wanted to begin therapy, along with Bliss Stone, with simple recognition techniques before progressing to other methods. My assistant was still questioning Rosemary's relatives and friends in another room. So I waited and contemplated.

Hypnotherapy is not an exact science. There are no rules, except perhaps experimentation. Some patients will respond to sound whilst others are stirred by odours, images, touch, and so forth. Some can never be persuaded. The trick for the therapist is to recognise what is not working before it has a negative impact on the session. Rosemary is already in an altered state therefore this kind of treatment is theoretically a waste of time. I began regardless.

'Rosemary, my name is Julian. Can you acknowledge my voice?'

There was no facial response. The victim continued to stare blankly, as if being pacified by an angel of death. The eerie lack of reaction indicated to me that internal happenings were all too active. I set up her personal belongings by the hospital bed. A storm was brewing outside. It was another hot, sticky day coming to an end.

'Jacob likes comic books.'

'So tell me, Rosemary, what type of comic books does Jacob like?' I asked and taped her eyes closed again.

My question was feigned and purely a twisted, light distraction. Rain pelted against the windowpane. Humidity is something that makes me feel uncomfortable and foggy inside. I moved towards the window and accidentally knocked over a silver tray and some flowers. I looked at Rosemary. Not even a hair was out of place.

I picked up the flower arrangement and recreated something resembling a lawnmower accident. I then moved towards Rosemary and removed the eyelid tapes from her face before placing more lubricant on her glassy eyeballs. I turned on my voice recording device and gently tilted Rosemary's head towards mine. My shoulders dropped, and I relaxed my entire being despite Rosemary's eyes appearing freakishly manufactured. My mind slowly detached from my physical awareness. The noise of the downpour faded in the distance as I slid silently into another reality of unrealities.

Searching for signs of activity in the mortuary of her gaze, I started to see some changes. I hung around for a bit and Rosemary invited me in. Her pupils dilated, and my vision absorbed her inky portals. Gazing hypnotically into a dark light, I felt as though I was crossing into the depths of Rosemary's mind.

This is another experience that will never make it into any medical journal, but it is better in your hands than that of the rule makers and naysayers.

'Jacob likes comic books,' I uttered. 'What else do you know about Jacob? Does Jacob know anything about you, Rosemary?'

The woman remained silent and the only sound I heard was the muffled tone of my own voice in another person's mind. In the abyss something moved, and I descended further. Impossible shapes inside the tunnel of thought passed through me and the images continued to roll.

I gave the cylindrical wall in my peripheral vision a colour. It was a hue of hazel, which might have been drawn from my visual memory of Rosemary's actual eye colour. I disappeared from the hospital ward and the hallucination imploded. Inward, further, deeper, an alluring bright dot bursting with activity wriggled. I have seen something similar to this before, but not through this kind of experience. A world so tiny yet larger than life was teasing me. I wondered if this is God's neighbourhood; the playground of our existence.

My ramblings continued.

'Jacob, Rosemary, biblical character and herb, spice, essence, spirit, God, the Bible, book, comic books, cosmic look, fantasy, hearsay, heresy, sin, purgatory, Hell, Heaven, good, evil, dead, alive, scripture, learning, church, deaths in church, only survivor, stuck in limbo, black magic, curse, sickness, stigmata, Jesus, crucified, blood, cure, separate, religion, God...'

I did not hear Bliss enter the room. She quietly watched the climax with the following words cutting the air: 'The Church! The Bible! Comic book! Torture! Death! Judas!'

Overwhelmed by an emotional deluge, I withdrew slowly from the inner world and deep, confronting sorrow. I swayed backwards as Bliss moved forward to prop me up. Instantly, a long buried personal memory of mine resurfaced.

I turned towards my patient once more. With pure exhaustion I said, 'I'm sorry. So truly sorry. Thank you.'

Emotionally fragile, I covered my leaking face with my big man hands. Bliss reached out to me in a state of bewilderment and gently pulled me from our patient's invisible powers and seated me near the door.

'Jacob likes comic books,' travelled across a sterilised room.

Through wet fingers I watched Bliss float towards Rosemary. Her long, ginger hair appeared to be dancing underwater. She taped our client's eyelids shut before returning to me. With her arm outstretched in a gesture of comfort, Bliss offered me something more than words. I declined.

We sat in complete silence and I eventually met her eyes. Bliss was certainly processing the situation the whole time. Playfully, she shoved my shoulder.

'Damn it, Julian,' she began. 'I know you're a brilliant therapist, but you're so ... something else too. I just don't know what.'

Bliss was trying to deliver a clinical blow, and it was good for both of us. I could easily love this child of a better God. We are stubborn, her and I, and we pretend to be stronger than we really are.

'I'm going to speak my mind, Julian.' Bliss inhales deeply and audibly. 'With all due respect, this isn't how a patient/doctor relationship is designed to work. You are blessed, perhaps even gifted, but lately you have been so caught up in personal bullshit that you fail to recognise the boundaries anymore.'

I took in every word the young professional delivered. These views needed to be spoken and heard. Disrespectful comments that are super accurate soften my heart. Somebody truly cares. I now wish to hand over my life to her; this scorching hot coal of an existence. Never before had I felt trust towards another human being on this scale.

'Judas likes comic books, Bliss,' I revealed cryptically.

'Jacob. You mean Jacob, don't you?'

'No. Judas.'

'Has the therapist become the patient?' Bliss asked.

I had never noticed the highlights in her fiery hair before or the fullness of her ruby lips in so much detail. The window behind her was the perfect studio backdrop.

'No. Yes. Perhaps?' I responded, confusing the situation even further.

'Julian, please concentrate. Who is Judas?'

There was no quick answer to her question. Judas is Judas. He is many things to me. From the darkest corners of my mind I move him into the light. The grieving process is always an irrational game. Bliss offered me an opportunity to express my grief. She waited like silence only knows how.

I strayed momentarily to absorb her boundless beauty again. She is a perfect distraction. I imagined the cruelty of God for creating Bliss Stone in such a flawless way, and equally cruel of me to think of her as flawless. This wretched hole I dig for myself is no place for angels.

However, without such angels in the pit, beasts like me will never get a glimpse of Heaven or the potential to rise.

I wish to finish Julian's chapter with my own version of events to remove the scattered energy he pencilled in his journal.

'Rosemary's situation triggered my own repressed memory,' Julian said. 'I thought Rosemary was lacking, but I am the tortured one.'

I pointed to Rosemary without looking in her direction. 'So this is all about you and nothing to do with that poor woman over there?'

'Not entirely,' he said. 'We can never be certain of what our patients can gain from us, or we from them.'

I asked Julian what he did know.

'I'm aware my Judas liked comic books; that's all.'

'This Judas of yours, who is he then?' I pushed against his reluctance to speak out. 'Where does he come from and where is he now?'

'My childhood,' he said from a cold place. 'Do you really want me to continue?'

'Yes, of course!'

My full attention was upon Julian, and we began the counselling session together whilst a patient listened in, or not.

'When I was nine I went to a strict boarding school. During my time there, I befriended a boy named Judas. He and I shared everything together, not that there was much to share. Despite this, I was fortunate to have exposure to my family home and other "worldly" material. Judas was less privileged. He had selfish, ruthless parents who never visited nor arranged for home visits. They donated heavily to the school and washed their hands of parenting altogether. Judas was withdrawn as a result. He found it difficult to mix with others, most of whom bullied him to no end. His only form of sanity came from my friendship and books. Not religious paraphernalia, but comic books that I had smuggled into the dormitory.'

'That must have been risky?' I assumed.

'We were flogged for not putting enough effort into our prayers. No one knew the consequences of bringing such "satanic pornography" into God's lap.'

Emotion gripped Julian again. He loosened a finger or two around his neck, and I silently encouraged him to keep talking.

'Judas was caught with the goods and...'

Decades of suppression had finally caught up to Julian. I underestimated the gravity of the situation. It was just a book after all.

'It was a long time ago,' I tried to reason. 'Not in your control any longer, Julian. Besides, at the very least you offered someone escape from the cruelty of loneliness and bullying.'

Julian absorbed my words, then I heard something truly ugly.

'Judas received a belting and was abused by our guardians thereafter. I too became the victim – and indirectly I also felt like the perpetrator. The guillotine dropped daily when the highest-ranking elders played pathological mind games with my friend. He separated himself emotionally from me, a coping mechanism perhaps, or maybe something more personal. It was I that handed Satan over to him after all.

'Judas's chair was often empty in the large dining hall, yet I knew all too well he was present. Our Principal Guardian sat at the far end of the dining area at a separate table facing all the boys. I understood, although I could not entirely grasp it at the time, that when the choirboys received dessert, Father Rolland's trumpet was being blown.'

Julian spoke metaphorically because he was trying to shelter me from the coarse imagery that described the scene, but I got the big picture.

'At first, I could not comprehend Judas's cryptic tales nor recognise the cries for help. After a while it became clear that during dinner he was fed scraps from Rolland's plate. He wore a collar and was held on a leash. However, during dessert Judas was expected to perform.'

Anger and toxic shock filled the room. I tried to keep it professional and personal. It would have been easier if Julian was only patient.

'That's so disturbing, Julian. I'm so sorry.'

'The organisation had parameters in place and the mantra was "Unity at all costs!" Older boys and even good-hearted Brothers with a conscience would share stories with certain students. I knew too much for a child and would seek and receive horrible details. We were all mice trapped in a cage and at any given moment the claws slipped through the bars slicing away at our innocence. It was a survival tactic to know all I could, even though I could not comprehend the full extent of the behaviour.'

Julian paused, and the treatment room became silent, as if the whole universe was listening in on our conversation. He glanced over at Rosemary and back again. I waited for a just ending to this horrible experience.

'One day I woke up in my dorm and stopped asking questions. I didn't care if God is the divine ruler of the universe or if He's a truck driver named Jack,' Julian explained.

'Why is that?' I asked.

'Judas died.'

I sat silent, as if death meant little in the whole scheme of things. On some level it felt like a comfort that Judas had died and left the human experience behind.

'Judas officially "slipped on a comic book", which apparently fell from the pages of his bible on his way down the staircase. He died from neck injuries at the scene according to internal investigations.'

'What actually happened, Julian?'

'I, along with other students, were present in his last moments. He was standing at the top of the staircase with a bible in his hand. He kept screaming "I am praying!" before Rolland arrived. He told Judas to come down immediately and to be more attentive to the call of God than satanic influences.

'Rolland started walking up the stairs. Judas cried out one last time as he approached. Judas stared at his abuser with such force that I felt the torture he endured over the years. He screamed with maximum hatred and pain, "I am praying, FUCK YOUR SOUL". Judas then ran and dived off the high platform, breaking his neck on impact.'

'No, Julian, no!' I reacted. 'And what about you and the other students?' I asked. 'For the trauma, did you get mental health support?'

'We were given counselling the religious way. It was focussed on scriptures and prayers to keep us on the straight and narrow. So we too did not fall victim to worldly distractions.'

I wanted to say a great deal to Julian and share my true feelings. Instead, I allowed time to pass before I continued further along the therapy road.

'Julian, are you suggesting that Rosemary's condition is based on your past and has nothing to do with the fact that she lost her friends in the massacre, or her son a year ago?'

'Rosemary is stitching up her own reality and this is how she searches for closure,' he said.

'Closure or denial? Look at her, Julian, it seems she is unaware of physical reality.'

'Whether Rosemary is fully aware of her external situation or not is unknown; however, I do recognise her refusal to be a part of it and therefore some kind of decision-making does exist.'

'What about you? What is your situation and how does that relate to our patient?'

'I can only reveal my experience, Bliss, and what you do with it is up to you.'

'Okay, so tell me.'

'Rosemary held the door open for me and I crawled in. I pushed my way through my barriers as much as hers. When the whole thing collapsed in on itself I entered a speck of activity and I saw them. The boys, Judas and Jacob.'

I adjusted my seating position. Julian pointed to a handheld monitor where Rosemary's child had been digitally placed. I stared at the image trancelike. I had seen Jamison (Jacob) before as part of the investigation, but now he seemed more detailed to me.

'What were the boys doing?' I asked.

'They appeared to be laughing and having a good time. I could not hear them, but they were standing in a featureless place; a dark backdrop much like negatives on an old film strip. Bright, inverted colours, but not ghostly. There was a lot of detail. As they flicked through a comic book, I gazed at them in wonder. Every so often they would look up and acknowledge my presence, sharing their smiles with me. That's all I could do, smile internally, that's all I needed for myself.'

'You know there are boundaries in our profession, Julian? I now know you're without them. You could have manufactured the scene of Judas and Jacob before going into your self-hypnotic state.'

'I unintentionally released my guilt by using Rosemary as a bridge between my past and present. I know that much. The brain inside each of us will always be a mystery to science because we cannot perform an autopsy on ourselves.'

'Your sofa has become all too comfortable, Julian, and your posture is suffering,' I remarked in a language mimicking his. 'It's certainly not mouthwash I smell on your breath too often.'

'Perhaps over time you will offer me a drink from your cup and together we could get the world drunk with our delusions,' he said, trying to lighten the mood and deflect the spotlight.

My response was safe. 'You ought to know by now that I'm always sober and in control.'

alien interaction

Julian was obviously a man of many emotions, various depths, and a system of complications. The following chapters reveal someone who blurs the line of multidimensional frequencies and then, despite being tone-deaf, tunes into it.

I've heard the 'insane' tell me the most rational theories. Those freaks have fragmented insights and are true artists of self development. People who insist there is nothing wrong with themselves are the most irrational of thinkers. There's no room for personal evolution without losing control in moments of fringe experiences. A greater intelligence than you or I always exists despite our frequency of denial and lack of clarity.

I've studied the unknown long enough to realise it's still unknown, no matter how much literature is available. Former illegal publications on the alien abduction phenomena – yes, as in extraterrestrial beings – hold my interest on many levels; however, I do not chase conspiracy theories, because that involves as much interpretation as dissecting the scriptures. There are too many variables and not enough time or passion.

Invisible love affairs are complicated. One begins to cling to ideals and is drawn in by soft notions full of promises. The conspiracy theories within each verse, photograph, or moving picture present aspects of alien capture which can appear evil for the most part. Humans seem to attach themselves and share bad news rather than good most of the time. This says something about our conditioning and our feelings of lack. I'm no longer frightened of this perception of evil because I refuse to subscribe to its inventor – mankind.

Many multidimensional shape-shifting beings can be retrieved under hypnosis. Therapists keep these alien creatures on a leash when patients recall certain blocked events. The danger is that hypnotherapy can produce false memories and sometimes interferes with the root cause of trauma.

The lure of extraterrestrials has bitten my flesh. These creatures have probed me, and I in turn probed their psyche. I have become infected by alien philosophies whilst man's DNA is being rejected. The longer I exist here, the more foreign this earth and its inhabitants are becoming. I find comfort in my 4am dreams, where I'm least vulnerable to human singularity and more tuned to multidimensional frequencies.

You might think my voice on this page speaks of fantasy. These are my secrets and of my disturbed friends in treatment. No rules apply. How do I tell my long-suffering patients who want resolve now, after years of abduction experiences, that there is no magic cure-for-all? There is a prejudice from those closed off to such night terrors. Human-on-human cruelty often surpasses any abduction experience in the long run. Put your flag down for a moment, your moralistic pride, and really think about that.

Unfortunately, most psychoanalysts are too busy rationalising to adequately listen and absorb. They prefer routine and safety, rather than interpersonal psychology methods. I allow myself to be mindfucked by the real emotional struggles that my victims have been persecuted for.

There are always questions that blister lips in hot debates. Are alien abductions real? Are they beneficial for the human race? Is there a takeover agenda? Are the chosen ones tripping on cries for attention after feeling raped by life? Is Heaven breaking every law of prophecy and every law of science too? Are the heavenly hosts the original caretakers of our planet? Is Jesus or Satan responsible? Everything random has a scientific equation; most scientists haven't figured that out yet.

Cults have flourished with the fear and love associated with our interplanetary beings. A subculture is rising. So much love; so much junk; so much fear; so many theories; so little evidence; yet so much concern.

Some abductees claim to recall regular visitations; others remember bits and pieces or nothing at all. That is, until hypnosis spurs the recollection. Then there are the good-versus-evil suppositions to contend with. Many abductees who originally found the ET experience positive have become repulsed and angry under hypnosis. The veil of their experiences lifts to reveal an unlikely bride, groom or creature.

The UFO phenomenon in recent times has become extremely profitable for savvy marketing agencies. Movies, streetwear, books, and other types of merchandise using ET faces are again in full swing. This subliminal shift into our consciousness via consumer goods has left the general populace immune to adverse reactions, whilst my patients continue to suffer sleep paralysis and mental disturbances.

I too experienced the kind of dreams that one might describe as 'night terrors'.

Although I've had undefinable encounters as a young child, sleep paralysis became more frequent after having my meltdown and changing professions. There is nothing out of the ordinary about sleep paralysis. These tricks of the mind seemed more defined and purposeful when I began to connect the dots on the universal radar, instead of a historic mud map. With my eyes opened, I remained asleep in these awakening dreams until I learnt to practice calm.

The feeling of paralysis is real, natural, and part of sleep during REM (rapid eye movement). If we didn't have immobility during REM, we could do some serious injury to ourselves, or others, as we act out our dreams. Sleepwalkers have a problem with this area of the mind. When we wake abruptly from our state of REM, our body can still retain effects of paralysis for around thirty seconds, although some sufferers claim it's actually more like minutes. Many of my patients indicated hours of paralysis upon their visitors' arrival.

The brain is still largely unexplored. In its depth possibly millions of lifeforms remain undiscovered. Unproven theories of parallel parasites and wondrous energy could all be in the mind, one way or another. These restricted zones can be blocked due to adult fears and pure ignorance. Thoughts can also be created due to preconceptions.

Everyone has a story in the closet, sometimes with unsettling characteristics that mimic that of another person's experience. So why do we tend to label it as 'just one of those things', a coincidence? Fears associated with cognitive processing is often the reason.

Other people's memories commonly overload me. Real or imagined, I initiated the desire to experience alien contact; to decipher fact from fiction firsthand. It has become one of my priorities to help those who are confronted by our otherworldly living arrangements. This would place me one step closer to something stealth, or quite possibly nothing at all. My experiences began alongside my mental instability.

Saturated in a cold sweat, I swam through an evening of familiar paralysis. I woke to see and feel the presence of two beings in my darkened room. One of them, a small creature similar to the popular 'Grey' classification, was instantly recognisable from pop culture. The other was not so easy to identify.

I was lying on my side, which is how I tend to sleep, and my body was locked in position by an invisible casing. The best I could do was let out a pathetic moan. The small alien was at the base of my bed before partially disappearing out of view towards my heel. I could make out its bulbous, silhouetted head by my feet against the curtains. My first reaction was fear, but then I noticed another taller being out of the corner of my eye, towering directly behind my head. Instantly I felt euphoric. I sensed he, a male energy, had been there for some time before I woke in this state. Acknowledging the tall being's presence took the edge off the primal fear, as if an element of trust had magically presented itself – maybe because he seemed to have a similar shape and energy to a human being, unlike the Grey.

The little shadow creature proceeded to do something to my heel, which felt hot although painless. I tried to stretch my neck to take a better look at the operating procedure. Crying out silently in my mind, I screamed, 'Let me see you; please let me see you properly!'

I could feel the taller being behind me was pleased by my enthusiasm. Nevertheless, he decided that it was inappropriate, perhaps too risky, to free my body. After much persistence, I slowly broke free of the invisible casing. My torso twisted slightly. Suddenly, without any sense of reason, my euphoria turned into fear. The effect of a drug had worn off. The visitors seemed annoyed and somewhat confused. Maybe because they hadn't expected me to move and weren't finished with their procedure, whatever that be?

A vibration of 'evil' pulsated through my memory glands, and then the experience cut abruptly like an umbilical cord at a birthing centre. I was physically freed from my nourishment provider. Dazed and bewildered, I was alone on my big bed again with no sensation of being watched or restriction. The only thing different was pure exhaustion. I immediately picked up my mobile phone and noted the time. It was precisely 4:11am.

In recent times my dreams are more detailed and complex. I can relive every frame whilst adding emotion and smell to the experience more often than not. These intruders/guests wake me at around the same time as other documented cases, usually just before sunup. I'm stereotyped, and I don't like that.

Challenged by my alien-like experiences, I continued to research documented cases of alien abductions. This only caused me further insomnia and a heightened vivid dream state. The sleep phenomenon continued. Recently I realised that my right thumb had become badly bruised and swollen after some kind of paralysis the evening prior. My thumbnail is now black with an obvious injury that I cannot recall. At the time, the pain wasn't enough to snap me awake.

Rationality is difficult when inundated with information far removed from our perception of reality. Sometimes we choose to believe unimaginable things because it is just that, unbelievable and exciting; a diversion from the boring routines in our lives. There is however always a risk to openly sharing experiences to a sheltered world.

Many abductees have psychiatric evaluations and are deemed clinically sane. In fact most live diverse and ordinary lives, if we look at the known medical statistics.

Heavy dreams continue in my sleepless comas. I no longer search for aliens, for they have finally found me. In turn, they have also found you and your reaction to them in this hedonistic journal.

Last week, at predawn, I was shackled to my bed again in familiar circumstances. This time my thought processes took a sharp detour. Initially, I woke with trepidation. My body in that rigid state much like previous experiences.

'Not again,' I thought. 'Not this time!'

I wanted to deny them, test them, and test me, Julian. In the 'now' moment, I remembered to be realistic about what was happening to my body. I slowed my reaction time to ingest the situation.

'Okay, I cannot move; okay, I can swear that someone is standing behind me. Okay, I feel a presence; it's okay, Julian,' I told myself, 'let your body relax and turn around without forcing it.'

The first thing I noticed was the shape of a larger being and a smaller one like before.

'Okay, are they really aliens?'

I turned in millimetres at a time. My body unlocked. I was aware as humanly possible that there was no missing time. All my limited movements and thoughts were systematic, linear and deliberate.

The tall alien came into view, then the smaller one. Again it was around 4am, happy hour, I was certain of it. I saw the distinct outline of my shoulder sneak up on me, and then my eyes followed the line down towards my hip and heel to comprehend the illusion of a little Grey in a dimly lit room. I began to smile, then laughed out loud. My muscles became fully relaxed and I had full bodily freedom with no air of strangeness. I was happy because I was either being played or I was playing with myself.

I tried not to impale myself with psychiatry because I didn't want my ego to make my decisions for me. Turning my attention towards the mentally ill, I followed their scent of madness. I love the humble patients more than I love myself, and they carry me when I cannot move forward in these opaque circumstances.

Although this bump in the night could be unremarkable, I cannot rule out all encounters to be the same. Many experiences seem so credible that it's difficult to find tangible explanations. My appetite for shape shifters continues to be insatiable. I long to experience unfathomable contact beyond my profession. And for all those Freudian textbook stiffs who link alien visions and out-of-body experiences to sexual abuse, or suppressed childhood trauma, try a little harder. By your logic all visionaries, artists, and great leaders who use other planetary beings to express themselves are the product of a broken home.

Some of the literature on alien interaction at my disposal is cheap and nasty. Many publications are far too poisoned with spiritual fantasy and not enough credibility. Within my stockpile, I do find some that have a sense of emotional honesty about them. A few of my clients could be within these pages, as I too might be one day.

10

agenda

There was more to Julian's entries than scribbles of a man losing his mind. I observed him almost daily, and one thing is for certain: he lived for his patients. He actually willed the unusual to manifest in his head, so he could be more beneficial to those who suffered through no fault of their own.

Following is the result of another visitation after a weekend of compulsive reading and heavy drinking, by his own admission. Julian immediately recorded the incident when he was capable. He wanted to ensure accuracy and give you the best seat in the house.

I was shooting down stars again in order to examine their mystery. This is reality within a dream, within a dream. I believe in such miracles.

I woke paralysed, and in my bedroom I felt a presence, yet nothing out of the ordinary was evident. It took a few minutes for my nerve endings to stop firing, causing me a state of anxiety. After breaking free of my frozen state, I shuffled through the lounge room and into the kitchen. I wasn't thirsty, but I drank a bit of water from the fridge anyway. There was a strangeness in this space, and the neighbourhood was soundless.

I directed myself back to bed after I poked my head in the nearby bathroom. Then I realised I hadn't checked my teenage daughter's old room, the spare bedroom technically, which had the door closed. Fully aware of current circumstances, I noted that Jacqueline had not visited me in well over a year. Regardless, I pushed gently on the door.

A small elongated figure was under the covers. My brain screamed for answers. All I received was alarming confusion.

Cautiously, my half steps took me closer to the edge of the bed. The lumpy layer was within my range of touch. I stood transfixed and waited for movement. The bed covers slowly peeled away at the head of the bed. The thing knew I was there. A few small fingers were visible and a face appeared in full view. I was expecting something ghastly, but not that.

A child, a boy of about six or seven, with a mop of sun-bleached hair was staring at me with a smug smile. All sense of logic reacted violently with the impossible nature of the situation. My initial concern was not for the welfare of the boy, he was safe, it was for me. The situation of someone else's kid in my home made me feel extremely uncomfortable. It would warrant intense scrutiny, especially when one considers my unit is located on the top floor of a secure building. No authority would accept that any child is capable of simply materialising into such an environment. Despite the sensitivity of the situation, I had a tremendous urge to contact the authorities, as if it was second nature. I raced over to my bedroom and picked up the phone. The moment I pressed the last of the three distress numbers, the signal died. I was not alone. The boy instantly appeared.

He stared at me with experienced eyes, this small child. There was a knowing that was elusive, and something exceptionally familiar about him. He looked at me as if to say, 'Why don't you recognise me?'

For a moment I felt awkward – me, the adult – in front of the child. I then got serious with the boy, but struggled to make him aware of the consequences his little prank could cause. I ordered him to allow me to call the police so he could go home to his concerned family. The boy's expression changed from one of confusion to a heavy heart. Something else was going on, and I couldn't figure it out – yet.

Uneasily, as if forced, he unnaturally smiled briefly at my latest observation. He knew my thoughts just as I felt his mood. He slammed the door of my room without touching it and was out of sight. It was at that moment I realised I could not move. It was like sleep paralysis all over again, but I was upright and fully alert.

After an enormous exertion of willpower, I peeled one foot from the sticky floor and then the other. My target was the other exit, a glass slider dividing my bedroom and the veranda, which was the nearest door available to me. The boy reappeared without disturbing the observable world of physics, and I didn't care how he did that trick. He seemed surprised I'd made it as far as I did. My calls for assistance sounded more like an annoying cat on heat than from a man in trouble. In all that time I had slid the glass panel barely a few centimetres whilst trying to access the outside world.

I pushed even harder with my mind.

'I AM THE ADULT!'

The spell broke. Pressure from my muscles released a backlog of energy against the metal door frame. A glass plate screeched along its tracks until hitting the rubber stopper on the other end. The whole structure tumbled over my narrow veranda, fatally crashing onto the pavement below. I peered down at the serrated tangle of glass and twisted metal, just to make sure it was real. I was well pleased. My neighbours would surely be awake now?

My calls for assistance fell on the hearing-impaired. Nobody responded.

'Where did that kid go?'

I emerged from my room and spotted the boy running into the laundry beyond the kitchen. In that instant my attention was diverted to the angry red light on the intercom and its annoying beeps. I pressed the button, releasing the lock downstairs without seeing who wanted in.

Three figures found their way to my apartment. Two men flashed identification cards at me, which I didn't study, and told me they represented some law enforcement agency. A thinner, taller gentleman, whom I considered to be the boy's biological father, accompanied the officials, but said nothing. The four of us stood in a circle near the kitchen.

The lofty stranger moved closer towards me. Immediately, I sensed he was the one controlling this entire situation, not the child. The detectives questioned me and I ignored them. Instead, I turned towards the father figure knowingly. He did not seem concerned about his son in the way a normal parent would. In fact, the child was not seen again and no search was even conducted.

A dimension beyond physically triggered events opened inside of me and I comprehended this was a test of some kind. I was in the presence of something special. This 'Nordic', although he could just as easily be Mediterranean, was totally in tune with my thoughts. He gathered the attention of the two detectives and cast a spell on them. They spoke in unison.

'Oh? You know your child is here? Well, there is nothing further to investigate.'

The law left with synthetic thoughts. All accusations vanished along with them. I was a model citizen in their eyes – despite their eyes being blindfolded.

Emotions not present earlier lifted me. This Nordic was reading me and giving me experiences, as if His civilisation was in the balance. He was too many life forms, and I didn't have the mental capacity to hold a conversation with all of them at once. I crumbled under the pressure. My heart belonged to all of them equally.

There was one Nordic and one me; there were multiple conversations, multiple elements of all things said and unspoken. No one was pulling my strings; I believed I was self-firing, self-aware that time.

I heard whispers of a confession and felt dirty. I witnessed a baby crying and felt helpless. I recalled a mother's love and felt touched. I experienced a zebra taken by a large crocodile and felt acceptance. I saw myself leap from a tall building and changed my mind when I reached the fourth floor.

I knew this Nordic, but never questioned how such a thing was possible. It was just a given. He stood in true stature like any other perfectly normal relative or friend. I saw no arachnid, no spider looming over me. He was not a tick causing me paralysis either. There was no sense of threat, no fear of lizard creatures or deceivers of man. I felt closer to nirvana somehow. I sensed a strong invisible connection and it felt natal. It felt like very early childhood.

I actually took notice of the Nordic's eyes. His whites were not visible; just a deep, bluish-black blend. He was taking on a slightly different form and continued to do so, but it made no difference to my situation.

I walked with him down the stairwell and commenced communicating with the powerful individual. I felt strongly about apologising – not for the bogus incident at hand, but regarding some other matter of great importance. I asked many questions and somehow he kept the answers at bay without offending me. Upon reflection, it could have been because I was creating questions for the answers I already owned.

Shards of broken glass were spread along the pavement and garden area of the common land below my balcony. I chose to walk on the sharp embers. A handful of people looked on in silent confusion in the hazy night air. My bare feet bled profusely. Glass shards broke and splintered under my weight. It felt like nothing at all. No pain, just simple appreciation.

There were many that walked this way to promised lands, and I never really understood why. They too must have felt numb in their hope of something greater than this existence.

The dread of not knowing how others must really feel was lifted. A question I never asked was answered. It was a reminder, a good reminder: I am only human. I am comfortable with that role for now and not expected to do something beyond my capacity as a physical spiritual being. I don't have to walk to the ends of the earth to find a cure to a disease of my own making.

The few onlookers dispersed, controlled, never to remember the incident. It was my time after all, not theirs. The stars had not yet melted into the dawn. The boy had not materialised, and I ad-libbed a forgotten script. Again, I extended remorse. I had something to be sorry about; conflicts of interest.

I knew things: fragments; truths; promises.

After self-assessment, my hand reached out to Him. Although this Being appeared to be male, it wasn't by total definition. As we walked back towards the street near my building's entrance, I rubbed His forearm, like a child reassuring a parent of his or her awareness of misconduct. I waited for endless forgiveness and looked into exposed eyes for confirmation. Those eyes, which many fear, had changed.

My Teacher's pupils were now two small dots. The whites of which were marked with different coloured lines, much like pen strokes on clean crisp paper. Blue, green, pink, and so forth. This Personage was a physical being with spiritual traits, not robotic or ghostly. He had unyielding personality like a respected school educator. A soul was unmistakable in His biochemistry.

This One was a loving educator trying to reteach me old lessons. I was a stubborn, although loyal, student who wanted to show submission and independence all at once. I wanted familiar habits and new tricks to live together. Lately though, I had lost all direction. It occurred to me that I was getting too headstrong; inevitably straying from a previous agreement we had aeons prior, or in the future.

Once more I apologised. It pained me for wanting to understand more than my capabilities. And I expressed regret for challenging the path that had been agreed upon, which I, and others, personally endorsed for this incarnation.

'Am I a traitor of some description?' I directed my thoughts to my visitor. 'You have to understand,' I explained with gut-wrenching emotion, 'it just gets extremely difficult and I don't know which way to go with it.'

I'm not sure whether He understood the term 'difficult' or if He was playing mind games again; however, I did feel an awkward form of sympathy towards my situation. I rubbed His forearm again and let my two minds run together in a huge field. I absorbed everything in my path whilst the silence of this witness watched my every thought.

I pondered why I was feeling so much overwhelming love for this Being. Then I questioned if He was generating this, or if it was me?

Despite becoming aware that I could withhold some of my thoughts, I simply didn't try. I was unconcerned whether my questions were open for discussion or not. Regardless of logistics, I felt obliged to help the cause, whatever that may have been, and in whatever capacity.

'You are a writer and your job is nothing more than to observe and record,' he shared. 'That is all you should be concerned about whilst you are here.'

The Nordic's logic did not rest on my shoulders comfortably. My shortcomings would make a mockery at such a flawed statement. My career as an author was nonexistent and unforeseeable. All I had was this personal journal.

My thoughts stopped dead, and then I asked him something from nowhere, verbally.

'What generation are you?'

In that instant I crystallised another fragment of information. He looked through me with his smooth, old face, whilst I allowed him to seek the things I could not find within myself. He had blocked his extrasensory perception from me, but I had something primitive at my advantage that he did not – a gut feeling.

'How could you guess such a question?' bled through. My inner being saw it as something relevant.

My mind's mind took me on another journey in that moment. He was different, this Personage, and a part of me was rejecting him whilst another accepted his genetic fingerprint. Every living cell within me split into a DNA spiral, further creating more fragments of the self than I could ever sustain in human form.

I felt swamped in shallow truths and deepening lies here on Earth. I wished to return home, if only someone could point me in the right direction. With a great deal of emotion, although He didn't physically show sentiment, we both gazed at one another for equal appreciation and respect.

It finally came when he said, 'Now we can talk.'

11

distinction

My Nordic friend had fled the scene. My hands were cold again. I have touched many corpses and experienced entities searching for warmth in my stiff body. When will these spectres learn that blood is just the oil that keeps our machines moving, not the heat source? And when will humans appreciate that apparitions cannot benefit from bloody sacrifices?

I woke to the sound of old people talking loudly around the pool. I looked down towards my feet expecting red sheets, but my wounds were miraculously healed by divine sunlight. I lay silent and tried to recover the highlights of my hypnosis. My memory didn't allow it. An insight I dared not reveal, not even unto myself, slowly bent my imagination. Pencil scribbles on a piece of paper resting on my bedside table drew my attention. I picked up the words and tried to recall the moment I wrote them down, but I couldn't get a visual. What kind of bender was I on last night? It was just one night, wasn't it?

I felt the desire to hold a sharp knife and deface every history book in sight. I felt the need to smash two crystals together and keep the dream alive long enough for the believers among you to stay warm in cold caves. I cannot reasonably estimate how many other eclipsing thoughts I had whilst outstretched on my bed, but it was the thought of the Nordic that eventually got me moving.

I washed the dead cells off my face to reveal the same person I had seen a couple of days earlier. I then walked into my kitchen, where I had earlier chased a strange kid, and poured a strong coffee in an adult sized mug before entering the spare room. I rummaged through some draws and found an old envelope. I took it onto the verandah – which did not have a glass door missing – and leaned over the balcony. Elderly people left the area as younger ones made a splash in the pool below.

My Nordic visitor shone a clear message in the murkiness of my mind. I wish I could tell you with certainty what that message was, but for now all I can do is pretend I know much more than you do under these circumstances. If you find it difficult to believe that great detail can be recovered from a dream, then see it as something other than a dream. We are all capable of hallucinating without being medicated.

That little boy who visited me during the night is actually me, in physical form at least. I'm looking at him this very moment in a photograph whilst writing this information down for you. My acupuncture of the mind is releasing some tension as I discover more about myself in a corridor without walls.

The supernatural being within us all is untouchable and individualistic. It remains out of bounds to any other force despite their influences. Your soul is impossible to penetrate because at the core of it you are not that fragile. Your existence is carved from frequencies that are invisible when you try to notice them consciously. We are an extension of something beyond our vision and we loosely call this thing 'God' sometimes.

I wanted to please someone, even you, because I couldn't please me. This someone appeared to overwhelm me in a state of bonding love. My uncertainty whether I generated that love, or if the Nordic did, still remains uncertain. Ultimately, though, God's symbolism never left me. Maybe the priest in me is talking now? Do I sound preachy again? Forgive me. This message flows and it is a river of many bends.

We inherit consequences based on choices. I chose to reject the physical, metaphysical, and spiritual boundaries when I faced this Nordic who appeared to live inside me. My physical reality only services my body and has nothing to do with my actual existence. This interaction was particularly important to me in my confusion. It separates me from you and assists my stagnant mind to open to greater things. This is, after all, a spirituality check in as much as it is a health assessment.

I've been impatient lately. Cathedral's workload is piling up and it's still not enough to satisfy me. I want to get inside more people's delusional minds so I can serve them better. Perhaps the fact that this Nordic mentioned me as a 'writer' has some significance? What better way to reach more people than to implement a system of mass hysteria over a few words? Do you wish to go on a pilgrimage to find yourself? Try remembering who you were before you had a need to be who you are right now. Are you confused? Maybe it's too confronting for you.

Have I fooled myself by creating my own world of conspiracies? We are all of the flesh. We create reality just as we create dreams. We always have. It would be selfish to ask for more and unfair to receive less.

The distinction between aliens, if any of them actually exist, and God, if He or She actually exists, and mystical life forms, if they actually exist, and me and you, if we actually exist, is universally important.

The real threat to civilisation is not some crazy dictator being exposed by another crazy dictator, for they are all playing the same pathological game. Tragedy comes from ignorance and missed opportunities that would widen the arteries and pump oxygenated love through our hearts. We mustn't attach ourselves to our past if we are to have freedom in the future. This idea is universally known; so what's wrong with our leaders?

I have reached a point in my spiritual maturity to question every inspired word. Cut and paste faiths reigned supreme in the old system, and I held the scissors and glue in that kindergarten. I am entertained for a moment, as I use my imagination to create God in my own image. Wow, watch Him struggle with the medieval minds of the modern age. Did I say Him? There was a time 'Him' was a 'Her', but that truth doesn't help a man who wants to be served by a woman.

So here I go again, from one set of values to the next, from one intoxication to the hangover. The church encouraged me to drink its vintage, and now I fall on my laurels and violently vomit until I have nothing left except the bitterness of salvation.

From one extreme to the other, I land in my current profession as a psychiatrist and leave behind the pain until the next wave of nausea hits me. I hate talking like this. This is not who I am. Not yet anyway. So here I'll stop the bleeding-heart sentiment and continue with my unfounded veracity.

12

bloodline

A tough month was behind Julian, and the road ahead was still avalanche-prone. Our patient, Rosemary, passed away, and Julian confronted his mortified inner child, and Judas, to make peace with them. However, other developments gained his attention and he had an opportunity to find out more about the living by asking the dead.

In one of our unguarded moments, G told me I was a good piece of clay in God's hands. I was not ready to hear it from a non believer, because even the believers don't believe they can ever truly measure up. My clay must surely be made of mud.

There is no reprieve to the static that hums torturously every day in my waking hours. Any sense of belonging is slowly peeling away within the yellow walls of Cathedral Haven. At best, the place offers variety, and at worst it offers variety also.

Along with the tortured individuals who pass through the system like lab rats negotiating a maze on their quest to find nourishment, only to be given a mild shock for their efforts, I push on senselessly.

One of my semi-regulars is a woman in her mid sixties. Lana Bullathakis is the mother of one of the non-medical staffers at the hospice. I never charge Lana for a consult, but I gain something from her supercharged energy despite her physical and mental setbacks. She actually reminds me of someone close to me whom I lost a few years ago.

Mrs Bullathakis had undergone repeated operations in a cat and mouse game to rid the spread of recurrent cancers. The woman's long-suffering body randomly rejects pills, injections, and inhalants. Synthetic relaxants and mind altering medications have proven vital for recovery to other patients, but Lana is somewhat of an enigma. The pollutants of chop-chop (illegal tobacco) attacking her clogged lungs continues to make matters worse.

By pattern recognition alone, it remains clear that Lana's mental state is poisoning her physical responses. This also causes a numbing effect in the hearts of those who love her unconditionally. I too feel the strain of unconditional love and have compassion for those directly affected by the attachment.

I'm aware that my therapy sessions with this grandmother are ineffective due to her constant mental congealing when improvements are made. She makes a mockery of my profession, and that pleases me because it keeps me motivated.

There is a long history of ferocious verbal attacks between Lana and her husband, George. I have witnessed the emotional language between them often, and yet their marriage remains a passive-aggressive union.

Perhaps I desired to be in amongst the turmoil, in the frontline as it were, to gain perspective. Or did something else motivate me altogether when I drove up their driveway for a casual visit?

Lana stood in the doorway of her house, resembling a ghostly skeleton clutching a coffee cup with a tight, bony fist. I could smell crude homemade cigarettes on her greeting kiss.

'Doctor Julian, please come in!' She pulled my wrist with her free hand. 'George! George bloody!' she blasted. 'Come ... George bloody, we have a guest!'

The elderly gentleman turned his head casually from his reclined position. The television screen was large and loud. I registered aging eyes, and almost instantly they bounced within centimetres of my face. His right hand connected with mine in a firm welcoming handshake whilst the left one rested on my shoulder.

'Julian,' he said. 'Nice you come visit.'

'Turn that thing down, bloody!' Lana shrieked. George raised his open hands to the ceiling and muttered something foreign before switching off the device. He then faced me with a broad, gappy smile and pulled on my arm to lead me outside.

'This way,' he directed.

'Why you think he likes your plants?' Lana asked. 'Let the man relax, bloody!'

George ignored the howling woman, and I noticed the vegetable garden appearing before us.

'What's your specialty, George?' I asked.

'I grow many things,' he said proudly. 'Spinach, tomatoes, broccoli, and cabbage usually grow best for me.' Before I could continue the conversation, George looked over my shoulder and yelled at the house. 'Lana, are you making coffee!'

'Yes, yes, what you think I'm doing in the kitchen, nails?'

I laughed lightly and then apologised.

'No, no, no, Doctor Julian.' George shook his head repeatedly. 'It's okay, we always talking like this. Normal for us.'

'I understand,' I replied.

I hadn't planned on staying for more than a quick chat and hot drink, but when a familiar visitor appeared on the back veranda it turned into a mini event. Their daughter, Sophia, and her young son, Alec, were staying for dinner, and I was invited to dine with them. It's difficult to refuse a meal with people of European heritage.

During dinner a dull headache of mine developed into something more serious. It continued to crush me until I could no longer contain it without losing my concentration. The severity of the pain mutated into a different kind of sensation that was becoming familiar of late. With nerves firing dry ice during every thought process, I struggled connecting my mind with my speech and began slurring my words. My disconnect to the moment did not go unnoticed.

'Maybe you are allergic to Lana's cooking?' George reasoned. The screech that followed did nothing to ease the increasing discomfort.

I saved my final ounce of concentration and walked towards my vehicle after inhaling some painkillers with no effect. Comparable to a drunk staggering out of a pub that has no duty of care policies, my ability to make appropriate decisions fell towards the kerbside. Fortunately for me and other road users, sensible company was by my side and I was led into Sophia's childhood bedroom.

With a cold pack over my eyes and drugs in my system, I drifted uncontrollably into isolated, crippling pain. My body was no longer attached and I was weightless; decapitated. The torture became unrealistic, and I found myself slipping in and out of sharp sensory awareness – somewhere between solar discomfort and the calming darkness of the room, and somewhere else bordering on numinous. Hours must have lapsed when I woke.

'Julian.' A whisper penetrated my cocoon. 'Julian,' it persisted.

The existence of a female presence behind the voice lingered as my confusion searched beyond the reach of my eyes. She was physically present behind my recuperating corpse on the large mattress. The bed had ample room for both of us, but I was on the very edge of it.

My vision was awash in total darkness. Gently, I rolled my torso and outstretched my neck, when my brain registered a shapely figure in the gloom. Processing the tone of her voice, I reasoned that she was asking for my permission to disturb this painful sleep. My mind adjusted to the experience, and the room illuminated. My sleeper's mind stirred into responsiveness.

She had no familiarity about her; young, slim, mid twenties, and attractive with copper-toned skin, which became more visible as the room produced more light from an unknown source.

'It's okay,' I mumbled. 'Stay. I'll be right.'

I turned towards the window to relieve the pressure in my neck. Without further prompting, the woman reappeared in full view beside the bed and looked at me directly. She waited silently for me to collect rational thoughts whilst studying my face. I fixated on her every detail, including her blue summer outfit from another era, which consisted of short shorts and a matching short-sleeved top.

My analytical mind gathered information before processing it unreservedly. This woman was a complete stranger, yet I couldn't rule it out completely. I moved and sat upright on the edge of the bed with the mysterious lady waiting for me to catch up.

'You're black!' lodged in my brain, as if it had important meaning. The woman did not actually have dark pigmentation; she had more of a Roma skin tone. I wished to withdraw the easily perceived slur and instead I repeated it.

There was uncertainty whether this lady could read my thoughts or not at this stage; however, no obvious offence was shown. I did, for whatever reason, believe she could gauge my heart condition. Despite this, I continued to beat myself up over the one-liner.

'I love you,' I declared audibly. 'I really love you! Do I know you?'

The visitor smiled. She remained silent and appeared to anticipate all the other bottled questions I shook and sprayed all around the room.

Lana frequently mentioned seeing 'a man in a black suit' in the house, but she could not get enough detail to identify the figure. She often sighted him walking away from her after feeling a presence. Lana also had other visions that could easily be categorised as an overactive imagination brought about by an unforgiving childhood.

This night visitor offered me an opportunity to expand my belief in grey matters. I never asked questions of trivia, like her name. I turned to my own existence and insecurities to strike up a conversation.

'How am I doing?' I asked, regarding my relationship with God.

'Borderline,' she responded instantaneously. The news was not exactly surprising. Then she added, 'You need to reduce your swearing, stop smoking and curb your drinking.'

'Huh?' I puzzles. 'I don't swear, much, smoke not at all, and drink, yes, somewhat.' My crystallised headache had slowed the process of understanding cryptic messages. The young woman waited patiently until I sent a thought bubble her way. 'You're not talking literally,' I finally comprehended. 'Have you been watching me for long?'

'Yes, we see what you're doing sometimes,' she replied matter-of-fact like.

I had opportunity to ask all about the spirit world, and it never occurred to me that it was even remotely as important as the other topic hunting me down.

'Why am I so consumed with alien activity in recent times?' The woman remained silent for some time. She shifted her eyes to a corner and held them there. I threw another question her way. 'Can you tell me anything about these beings?'

There was a heaviness of uncertainty, perhaps even concern, in her voice. She looked back at me with an empty stare.

ACUPUNCTURE OF THE MIND

'No. Not really. They are on a different schedule. Not much is known. I don't really know... when some people go with them they aren't seen again.'

Could the meaning of life get any more complicated? What was I supposed to do with that? This came to me almost immediately:

'That's logical. After all, if alien species live much longer lives than humans – up to 20,000 years – and are capable of extending human life into the thousandth year, then it remains consistent that a recently deceased individual, taken or otherwise, will lose contact with loved ones.'

My visitor responded with diluted expression. She could certainly hear my thoughts. Surely she didn't need time to digest my overactive reasoning? Or maybe it was simply a reaction to an incorrect assumption? Either way, I had to work it out myself.

I then shifted the conversation to Mrs Bullathakis.

'Why don't you reveal yourself to Lana and put her at ease?' I asked.

'I cannot do that,' she insisted.

'Why?'

'I refuse.' She moved her head towards the direction of Lana's room and scowled.

A shuffle in the hallway diverted my attention, and I noticed another kind of light source between the door and floor. The young beauty faded slowly. This was the first time I noticed her in this form, as an ethereal entity.

'Don't go!' I pleaded. 'Please let her see you at least this once.'

Personal validation of a sighting was never my motivation. I don't care for such trivial triumphs. All I wanted was to ease Lana's torment a little because she is the one that truly believes and wants detail.

'I really have to go now, Julian.' She blended into nothingness. I lay down in my sleep position moments before the bedroom door gently opened. My head throbbed, and my carer checked up on me like a mother would her sick child. I pretended I was asleep until I fell into it for real, pain and all.

Upon waking my head was still throbbing. Although manageable, I eventually moved down the hallway and followed the magical aroma of coffee.

'Julian love, how you feel?' Lana asked, as she extended her cold, thin hand and wrapped it around my wrist. She squeezed my flesh affectionately.

'Better,' I replied, mentally preoccupied. The early morning event was still strong in my conscience.

'What is it?' she asked. 'Something wrong?'

'No, not wrong. Can I meet you out on the back patio, Lana? I just need some air.'

'Of course, love. I'll bring coffee. Do you want whiskey in it?'

'No thanks, just black with one sugar.' I smiled politely.

George was already out of the house. He had a doctor's appointment almost on a daily basis. He was chasing the latest ailments. I would have prescribed time out from his wife, but it wasn't my place.

Lana sat across from me, after placing an assortment of biscuits on the table, and handed me my coffee. She met my stare. 'Okay, love, what do you want to tell me?'

'Firstly, I wish to thank you for your hospitality and taking care of my needs last night.'

'This is nothing,' she replied.

'I value that you have a lovely home and nice family.' Lana's face showed signs of genuine pride. My words kept flowing without consideration for doctor/patient etiquette. 'I just want you to know that I had an experience last night and I do believe you. Do you understand what I mean by that?'

'What? You mean you saw him?'

'Everyone sees things at times, Lana, for different reasons,' I explained. 'This does not necessarily indicate that these things are of a real nature.'

'What did you see, Doctor Julian?'

'I had a dream last night. A young woman came to speak with me and –'

'A woman? What did she say?'

'It's what she didn't say that I find interesting,' I confessed.

'You confuse me.'

'I will explain. First, tell me if there is any reason why a darker-skinned, pretty, young woman would be hanging around?'

'No. I don't know any person dead like this. What did she tell you?' Lana asked.

'I asked her why she did not appear to you. She expressed her refusal based on a grudge of sorts.'

'Grudge?'

'Yes, a feeling of resentment or dislike.'

'Dreams sometimes make no sense,' Lana deflected. 'You had a really bad headache last night and a high temperature too.'

'Yes, of course,' I concurred, stopping short of unveiling other experiences of a similar nature. 'It was a difficult night.'

The conversation diverted to other topics, and I enjoyed another cup of coffee in the morning glow. On my drive directly to work, I refused to question the rhyme or reason of the lucid dream. However, three days later I received a video call from Lana in my office.

'Do you have a minute, Doctor Julian?'

'Yes of course, Lana.'

'You were right. It is a woman!' Her excitement level rose sharply, and she spoke faster without pause. Some in my profession would look for signs to have her medicated, but I saw nothing except normal expressive behaviour.

'Did you dream her?'

'Yes, I think so. I don't know.' Lana shrugged her shoulders. 'She did not want to say anything to me, and I got angry with her. Then she said they came to see George. I look and see ghost people everywhere inside the house! I know they are his relatives and –'

'You think the young lady is related?' I interrupted.

'Yes, she is. I told George your dream the day you left and he said he had cousin who died many years ago. Sounds like this girl. Some of his family have darker skin. I don't know his family well. We moved lots after marriage and lost contact with many on George's side of family. Not sure why, just like that.'

'Does it really make sense to you, Lana? I mean, does it explain why she does not want to talk with you?'

'Yes, and they all disappeared after the girl told me why they are here. George is a good man,' she admits. 'This girl wants to protect him.'

'From who?'

Lana was silent for a moment and then said, 'Me.'

'What does that tell you about yourself?' I asked.

'I need blame nobody, specially my George, for problems in me.'

'That sounds logical to me, Lana. That's a strong thing you have considered. Maybe it's time to abandon old experiences and start behaving differently?' Lana glowed with enthusiasm. 'Your family loves you, and you need to love yourself too if you want Sophia, Alec and George to feel happier in your company. Put all this positive energy into healing your body and remind yourself often that your life is one worth living.'

Lana's eyes held tears of genuine human emotions. I said goodbye and disconnected on that positive affirmation.

13

sexual being

Male midlife loners: are they all tuned into the same frequency? Do they all have self-destructive characteristics? That's a fair question to consider as we enter Julian's next entry.

Conversation during dinner was most revealing. I had no idea I could be so entertaining and pathetic. Unfortunately, nobody was present to share my wit or challenge my intellectual flaws.

My apartment has little charm. It's the best a busy loner can do without faking his personality. There is a swimming pool in the courtyard, as you know, and I sometimes use it late at night to avoid awkward conversations with my neighbours. My weekends mirror one another. My refusal to socialise with other nocturnal singles is my way of proving to the world that I'm not desperate for emotional or physical approval.

My home-alone weekend was sideswiped by Jacqueline's phone call. She updated me on her intentions to extend her spiritual pilgrimage overseas with her mother a little longer. Another year or so is mentioned. My status as Dad is non-existent now. Mary and

Jacqueline are locked in a foolproof safe, and I have long since forgotten the combination of the box I built. It's easier this way. I would, if I could, do anything for Jacqueline, except abandon my core self and pretend that all is well in her mother's dogmatic world. I'd rather she hate me than love me with conditions attached.

Memories of my old persona, Father Julian, and his absolute trust in the eccentricity of the church cling to me like a blood-soaked soldier's uniform. The comradeship, the patriotic lifestyle, where one never questions the line of command, now sits naked and free. Nothing is left to the imagination any longer. I'm unable to meet the demands of yesterday's fears and would rather create my own world of illusions than conform to someone else's.

'Dear God,' I begin to mumble awkwardly, almost embarrassed. He is becoming a stranger to me now. 'Never mind.' I take another shot of whisky.

Why do I persist in trying to have a relationship with something I can never be certain exists whilst I'm still breathing? This is my true conscience trying to wake the sleepwalker who thinks he's awake in this moment with you. We are both very much asleep, you and I. Pinch me after the next few paragraphs and then you can tell me who is dead and who is alive.

The following experience happened shortly after my last feeble attempt at fighting physical limitations. I'm not proud of it. However, it taught me something about making assumptions.

Restlessly, I spread my naked, clammy body across my big, empty bed. For an hour or two I wrestled with the sheets and sought sleepy comfort without success. Emotional torment had me by the jugular. Bliss Stone entered my mind sexually, and the priest within tried to remove her image by calling upon angels to blur out her face as a sign of respect. That didn't last long. Within a deep breath she was standing before me half-clad. I rose from my tangled sheets and washed my burning face with ice water from the fridge. In the soft light bouncing off the kitchen window the baptism was being witnessed by invisible acumen. I stood fearlessly, as no amount of holy water could ease the symptoms of this human on heat.

A second attempt at sleeping eventually sent me out of my body. I drifted intentionally through my building's physical shell and knew exactly where my will was taking me; a sixth floor unit in another suburb. I elevated above the lower floors and entered the known structure via a closed bedroom window. Even the air-conditioner in this room did not cool me down. There was no silver cord restricting my movements nor did I care if I had abandoned my shell forever. Bliss slept alone. I admired her natural beauty like a stalker for some time. I waited for her to detect my presence and stir naturally.

She began to squirm, shifting her arms down one side of her body and then the other, before resting them on her belly. Bliss mouthed words I chose not to hear. My soul expanded into the portals between a fleshy world and one that literature has never accurately depicted.

The realness of my experience dissolved into the confines of my body when I woke prematurely. My sheets were saturated and beginning to form a crust. I ripped them off my mattress and walked into a soft shower and questioned my acceptance of the illogical. It seems my entire being is turning into a neurotoxin changing the molecular structure of my physical cells.

As the sun crawls across my tiled floors, I sip on morning dew and change the lighting conditions of my experience. Was this simply some form of mutated fantasy brought on by sexual frustration? My ego informs me that my sexual being is capable of seducing Bliss. I display dominance, sensitivity, vulnerability, and mystery. What young woman wouldn't want that? Okay, there might be some holes in that statement. I'm not irresponsible enough to light this candle and burn the house down.

As a man, I recognise the conflict celibate priests must have; a deprivation that could lead to depravity. I find it difficult to comprehend why any man dedicated to God in such a way should be trusted with young children or emotionally starving adults. Priests have genitalia and sexual desires too, just as their God had intended.

Many people claim sex is overrated and yet the sex industry is the largest on earth next to religious paraphernalia. The Bible sits on bedside tables, whereas vibrators hide in underwear drawers and porn is hidden in every electronic device. Sex appeal sells everything, including God and the perfect personification of a sexy Jesus figure, and to say sex is overrated would be denying life as a holy experience. Nature is one huge sex machine and the most important element of species survival. Even fertilisation clinics require sperm to be extracted sexually, usually with the aid of pornography. Consensual sex is healthy for the soul. I lack sexual drive at present, as my energy is diverting its power into areas of self discovery. For this reason, I'm grateful for my load of washing this morning. It's almost time for work.

I caught Julian at the office that morning. His stance was somewhat rigid; his jaw muscles were visibly tight.

'Miss Stone.' His greetings were not usually this stiff and I knew it was going to be a rough start. 'What are we in for today?'

'The usual,' I replied. 'Trauma, trauma, and more trauma.'

'Let's start with you then.'

'What do you mean, Julian?'

'I know a little about people,' he said. 'You are people, so what's on your mind?'

'Nothing important,' I replied. 'Are you trying to deflect something back onto me? We have patients waiting and I really don't have the desire to talk in riddles right now.'

'Really? When someone says "nothing important" it usually means they need to resolve something, but lack the commitment.'

Julian persisted and I knew it would only get worse if words were not spoken.

'Please don't analyse me, Julian. I simply had a stupid dream and I've been awake ever since,' I revealed. 'I'm just a bit tired, that's all.'

'Y'know dreams can reveal plenty about our general wellbeing.'

'I'm an intelligent woman who doesn't need to be guided into logical conclusions, Julian,' I lightly retaliated. 'I know you won't let this go until I talk, so let's get on with it before moving on to real patients.'

'What happened last night, Bliss?'

'Here goes... I woke up and immediately sensed someone was in the room. At the front of the bed a silvery hue illuminated my window. I felt the intense energy of this thing as it formed into shape.'

'Were you frightened?' he asked.

'Not at all,' I replied. 'I recognised the energy as something non-threatening, but couldn't place it in our world.'

'Intriguing. I'm keen to know how it turned out for you, Bliss.'

'Well, this light formed a human shape. It had no recognisable features. Now I don't even know how it's possible, but I recall my observations clearly.' I paused and thought about what I was going to tell Julian next, but what came out of my mouth was not it. 'It was you, Julian, and you know it was.'

'Of course you know it wasn't really me,' he said. 'You placed a face to it so your mind can relate to the experience somehow.'

'No, Julian. You wanted this conversation, and you got it!' I replied. 'Definitely you in some wacky form,' I insisted. 'I watch you go beyond the physical limits of the mind with patients and visit places that aren't visible in our reality. I have a feeling this dream is somehow related to an experience of yours and you willed it to happen. I was simply your tool.'

Julian leaned back, rested his buttocks on a table, folded his arms and looked down at his feet. I was watching the time and he was somewhere else, not in the present.

To finish this chapter, I will hand you back to Julian and his recollection of what happened next. This is about him after all, and I don't want to sugarcoat his experiences by pretending I know what goes on in his head in such situations.

As a very young child, my mother threatened to tie me up to the letterbox, naked, when I was misbehaving. It was an extremely vulnerable feeling. Bliss Stone was now leading me to the letterbox and it was not to check the mail.

'I felt your sexual tension,' Bliss continued. 'I could also sense you understood this behaviour was inappropriate, amongst other things. I guess I was willing to meet your demands and allowed you to dominate the situation, just as you do in your occupation.'

'Our brains store memory from our daily interactions.' I began to reason from a medical standpoint, which is rare for me. 'True, I have not been with a woman in some time, but –'

'Please, it's okay,' Bliss interjected, 'I don't need a rebuttal. Don't give it another thought. I understand you make perfect sense theoretically. I also know you are protecting yourself from me, and other women. Although I question your actions sometimes, I don't judge you, as I hope you'll never waste that energy on me either. There are obviously many factors involved here and we'll just let it be an experience that needs no further explanation.'

Bliss has incredible intuition, whilst fear stops me from allowing her the full credit she justly deserves. I guard my hollow lies and let nobody deflate them, especially someone so close to my heart that it causes me discomfort. I question if it was Bliss who held the energy last night, and I was simply a moth making my way through a dark evening of challenges. Sometimes I feel she is fighting my battles for me and I keep taking her weapons away.

I'm showing trust towards another human being again, and it continues to make me feel extremely uncomfortable.

14

Bruno

Bliss handed me a digital reader containing our daily patient list. I noticed Jasper in the line-up and the words 'Lactose Tolerant' next to his name. He is not considered a critical priority; however, he offers an opportunity for me to tap into forms of therapy I rarely practice. Jasper also delivers a form of inappropriate amusement due to the way he delivers his words and speaks earnestly about his experiences. Our client is a thirty-eight-year-old male who has developed a habit of hitting on lactating mothers – several at any given time.

A court decision had ruled Jasper to undergo psychiatric treatment after a few women filed a lawsuit against him. He usually charmed vulnerable, pregnant women and breastfeeding mothers. His addiction is baby's milk at the source. His fetish only became a root of anger for the women involved after their milk had dried up. He broke many hearts along his breast-milk trail of seduction.

The most pressing assignment of the day was the one I labelled 'Power Socket', which was the first session to tackle on our list of duties.

Bliss walked with me along the corridors of Cathedral towards our office. My focus was diverted to a nurse assisting one of our former trauma patients, Bruno, who was involuntarily caught up in a prison riot two years earlier. He had witnessed a guard kill his cell partner during a violent exchange. The last words his cellmate gargled before his death, which Bruno revealed to me under hypnosis, were: 'I see no fucking light. There is no fucking God. Darkness... Scary mother fucking darkness.'

These comments tortured Bruno on a deep psychological level. He grew up in a religious household that believed in the afterlife and a merciful God. Despite doing time, Bruno is a benevolent man who was imprisoned for a continuation of relatively minor crimes of association. His intent was never to hurt anyone. Some prisoners lack the education of being their own person and therefore gravitate to gangs in order to feel important. Prisoners, such as Bruno, would be better placed in psychiatric re-education programs to strengthen their resistance to gang memberships rather than punishment cells, which tend to reinforce they are unfit for society.

After the death of his cellmate, Bruno became chronically frightened of the dark and would scream uncontrollably after lights out. The prison guards thought that perhaps a small dreary cell in solitary confinement would fix the phobia. That's when Bruno really showed strong signs of his internal terror. He repeatedly bashed his head against the metal cell door to escape his demons. He cracked his skull on several occasions. Bruno eventually made his way to us as a temporary rehabilitation measure.

Gradually, I repositioned his blind spot. It took enormous endurance to demonstrate to Bruno of how the light for some would remain dim until their preference for violence diminishes. His former cellmate, Andy, was clearly a violent man and remained in darkness till the end. Bruno and I established that only individuals hell-bent on causing pain would manifest pain in this life, and beyond, because that is what they choose to respond to.

Bliss observed my sessions with Bruno and candidly told me that my methods were suggestive and extremely self absorbed. She is right, of course. Realistically though, the fellow is a simple man; a terrified long-suffering one whose only vehicle to inner calm is artificial injection of thought that comes from my own tribulations. There is little choice sometimes, especially if the alternative is routine mind-numbing medication and ineffective protocols.

'What happened to your feet?' I asked the wheelchair giant rolling in the corridor.

'I jumped on a fence.' Bruno's eyes opened wide like a wild eyed Pug.

'How do you jump on a fence?' I challenged.

'From a window. How else?'

'Of course, how else?' I nod. 'How badly hurt are you?'

'Not much.'

The aiding nurse stepped into the conversation to clarify the order of events.

'Our patient was pinned to a metal picket fence. Four long spikes passed straight through his feet and shattered his bones and tore ligaments and flesh. He was found standing on the fence, holding his balance with one hand against the building.'

'Ouch!' Bliss gasped. Bruno looked up at my colleague and shook his head side to side. 'That must have been extremely painful for you.'

Bruno rolled his eyes as a grin formed on his lips. 'It didn't hurt much. That's all the way down there!' Bruno pointed to his bandages.

All the way down there. If only we could all separate our pain in this simplistic way. The nurse smacked her palm on her forehead, then patted the convalescent on the shoulder and pushed ahead. Bliss and I moved on too. One of our most disturbed sufferers was no doubt anxiously waiting in our reception area for an extremely difficult treatment.

15

power socket

Many of our clients burn themselves at the stake because they cannot recognise what crimes they committed. They assume a guilty verdict due to their treatment and hand out their own punishment accordingly. Bliss and I have a responsibility to identify the perpetrators who helped set these victims alight. It's unfortunate how the profession of psychiatry can hinder the rehabilitation process sometimes, because we are too busy analysing rather than experiencing.

Much to my colleague's displeasure, I often push my therapy sessions firmly against a wall until either I break the wall, or the wall crushes me. I cannot protect all my patients from the rubble and they are fortunate to have Bliss do some of the heavy lifting for us.

'Welcome, Nadia,' I sensitively greeted. 'There's no need for formalities here, so please call me Julian. This is my colleague, Bliss.'

'Hi, Bliss.' The woman was fidgeting with her discoloured handbag strap.

Bliss reached out to touch the patient's trembling hands. She tried to put the woman at ease with a soft touch and gentle voice.

'You needn't be uncomfortable with us, Nadia,' she said. 'We are only here to help you.'

'Yes,' I added, 'and if at any time you wish to end our session, or if you are overwhelmed, please let us know and we will put the stops on.'

The patient acknowledged my statement with a slight nod.

'Do you have any questions before we begin?' Bliss asked. 'Any concerns at all?'

'No, I've been through this with other therapists,' the thirty-three-year-old divorcee replied. 'I just want to end this nightmare.'

'We understand,' I stressed. 'We'll begin with the medical notes and confirm our information before going any further. Please tell us if the following is a true representation of your history. According to our records you have been experiencing night terrors since puberty. You noticed a pattern coinciding with your menstrual cycle's most fertile time, around two weeks after your period begins. Apart from that, other random attacks are presented also. Is this correct so far, Nadia?'

'Yes, but my gynaecologist has found nothing too unusual, except for minor unexplained scarring. But it's not just the nightmares that concern me. Did the other doctors tell you about the flashbacks, sudden vision loss, short-term memory loss, unexplained bleeding, bloating and –'

'Nadia, please slow down, love,' Bliss intervened. 'We have plenty of time to make sure you get the best care. All your records are here, and, believe me, we are extremely thorough.'

'We understand how this seems like a roundabout to you,' I added. 'Please trust our directions so we can help you find an appropriate exit.'

Bliss offered Nadia a small oxygen mask with a relaxing fragrance, but she politely declined.

'We do things differently here compared to other practices,' I continued. 'We are more interested in pattern recognition rather than the definition of symptoms right now. That's how we separate the lollies from the rocks, so to speak. Do you grasp this on some level, Nadia?'

'Yes, Julian. I heard something about your methods here, something different,' she said without elaborating further.

'We will do all we can, I promise, but we need your input,' I stressed. 'The only way to achieve success, and I want to be firm about this, is if you are willing to open up to the suggestions I make. You have to realise that hypnotherapy only gives opportunity to self-hypnosis. Without your willingness to commit to the procedure there can be no chance of resolve. Do you fully comprehend what that means, Nadia?'

'Yes, yes I do.'

'Are you ready?'

'Yes.'

'What's the first thing you see when you get these flashbacks or night terrors?' I asked.

'A power socket,' Nadia responded immediately. 'That's all I ever remember. And there's an all-consuming evil presence that is thicker than any air I've breathed.'

'How do you feel emotionally when you see this power socket, exactly?'

'Terrified beyond belief.'

'How big is this power socket?'

'I can't really say, it's all I see. Huge!'

'Can you please inform us when you had your last period?'

'I'm at the end of it now,' Nadia replied.

104

Bliss assisted Nadia on the couch and propped us some cushions. Her feet were slightly elevated, and she settled her back and shoulders into the fabric.

'Nadia, I just want to be clear about your description. Is the power socket you see in these episodes of distress the old kind, or another type altogether?'

'The old style. It looks like it's made of aged plastic,' she affirmed.

'Are you comfortable, Nadia?' Bliss asked warmly. 'Shall we begin?'

'Yes, ready.'

Nadia Cape appeared relaxed, blinking her eyes in readiness for her morning session to commence. My pre-hypnotic suggestions were easily attainable, and Bliss coordinated the imagery with fragrances where possible. The subject was not exposed to any sense of threat, for now.

I woke the child who resided inside Nadia's adult life and found her building sandcastles on a gently lapping beach. Bliss placed an open bottle of coconut oil behind the subject's head. Nadia was unaware of her dramatic future; a life where she would be placed on suicide watch and suffering through repeated self-mutilations.

The woman in treatment is bald for her own protection. The temptation to pull clumps of hair and skin from her patchwork scalp had to be resolved. Her nails are also kept short. She is blind in one eye after stabbing a sharp pencil through it in a final bid to remove an image after her eighteenth birthday. Celebrations had become nonexistent, for they are particularly distressing. Many of her scars share the same anniversary date from a very young age.

'How do the waves feel on your feet, Nadia?' I casually asked.

'It tickles.'

'Who else is at the beach with you today?'

'Just Mum.'

'Where is your father?'

'At work.'

I directed Bliss to cap the suntan lotion and ready the next item to help with hypnotic approach.

'Okay, Nadia, you are a few years older now, a young teenager. Your body is going through some changes, which is important in every young girl's life. This is totally natural and necessary for adult development. Do you know what I am referring to?'

'My first period?' Nadia's tone changed significantly.

'Are you afraid?'

'Nup! I've been wearing pads for three months already.'

'Why is that?'

'Because all my friends got theirs before me and my first one will be here soon.'

'How old are you, Nadia?'

'Almost fourteen. In a couple of weeks actually.'

The fragrance of wattles in bloom filled the office space quickly. The research Bliss conducted into Nadia's family's rural property shows the area was awash with wattle trees. Our subject was responding well so far.

'Okay, Nadia, now you're having your fourteenth birthday. What's it like?'

'Great! I'm getting all grown up stuff like makeup, perfume, and a new smartphone!'

'Is it a big party?'

'Yeah, and Jess and Alison are sleeping over tonight.'

'That sounds like fun,' I commented and move onto more personal matters again. 'Now Nadia, when did your first period begin?'

'That's a strange question to ask,' she protested. 'Didn't you ask me something like this before?'

'This is important,' I insisted.

'If you must know it was a couple of weeks ago, actually.'

'Okay, thank you. All your party guests have left, except Jess and Alison. What do you and your friends do now?'

'We talk and go online.'

'Where are you talking?'

'In my bedroom.'

'Are you all sharing the same bed?'

'No, they are in sleeping bags on the foldouts.'

'What do you talk about?'

'Boys.'

'Anything in particular?'

'Well, if you must know, Alison let Angus touch her boobs and she felt him go hard.'

'Okay Nadia, thank you. Do you stay awake talking all night, or does everyone fall asleep?'

'I fell asleep after Jess.'

'Okay good, Nadia. Now enter your dreams. Tell me what you see.'

'I don't dream anything, but I'm awake again.'

'Nadia, what is it that you see when you are awake?'

'Two holes.'

'What type of holes?'

'Big power socket holes.'

'Can you see your friends?'

'No.'

'How do you feel?'

'Kind of mixed up.'

'In what way? Tell me all your feelings. It's okay, you are safe.'

'I feel trapped, loved, sexually stimulated, used, needed, abused. I hate it here. Get me out of here!'

'You are safe, Nadia, I am nearby. It is very important that you continue to explain to me what you are experiencing. Where are you?'

'I don't know,' she concerned.

'Can you move?' I asked.

'I don't think so. My brain says I can, but nothing works.'

'Nadia, I want you to look up above the power point and tell me what you see.'

'I see a smooth wall that looks like metal and glass mixed together. It's so strange looking.'

'That's good, Nadia, now turn your vision to your right and tell me what you see.'

'I see another power point.'

'You are doing great, Nadia, now what do you see on your far left?'

'I see another power point.'

'You are safe, Nadia. Now you must look towards your feet and tell me what you see.'

'A funny bright light.'

'Why is it funny?'

'It's so bright that I can't see anything else there, but it doesn't hurt my eyes or shine like other lights.'

'Okay. Nadia, now I want you to relax deeply and ask your feet to move gently and take a step backwards.'

'I'll try.'

Nadia took a moment then became increasingly distressed.

'What is it, Nadia? What's going on?' I asked. 'Step back and tell me what you see.'

'I can't step back,' she responded.

'Why not?'

'There's a wall against my back! I don't like it here. I want to go home and be with my dad! I'm scared. Please get me out of here!'

'You are a very brave young lady, Nadia. Do you think you can manage just one more thing before returning home?'

'No!'

'Please, this is most important.'

'Okay, but hurry!'

Nadia's agitation was distressing to observe, even for seasoned therapists; however, I felt compelled to push the needles further into her psyche and find the most concealed areas of pain and conflict. I could sense Bliss had serious concerns about my conduct and Nadia's well-being, but that did not stop me from injecting more of my own poison into the situation. I was beginning to identify the source behind Nadia's lost suffering and the only way to get it out was to get in deeper.

'Nadia, simply shift your eyes to one of the power sockets and hold your gaze,' I instructed.

'I don't want to,' she said before a long silence. 'SHIT! No no no, help me!'

'You are safe, Nadia. You have the power to break the connection between the power socket and your personal space, but you need to let it know your intentions first. Nobody, or anything, can stop your will to do what it wants!'

'I can't...'

'Nonsense! You can! You are your own person with your own boundaries. Are you looking directly at the power socket?' I asked for confirmation. 'Look at it, Nadia. Are you looking at it?'

'Yes, but it's so powerful and now I can't look away.'

'Yes you can, Nadia, listen to my voice and follow my instructions with all your concentration. Blink three times and shift your eyes below the two holes.'

Bliss and I watched Nadia's closed eyelids twitch.

'Look down, Nadia. What is it that you see?'

Nadia began to sob.

'You are in control and you are safe, Nadia. What do you see beneath those power sockets?'

'A tiny hole; a mouth. I see a mouth with no lips... I don't understand ... Daddy?'

I gently brought Nadia's boiling distress back to a simmer and then let it cool off with words of encouragement and adult strength.

'You are safe, Nadia. You have done really well. You are in control of every situation, including this one. No harm will come to you. You are falling back to sleep quickly and you are safe in your bed, in your family home, with Jess and Alison. Your friends are starting to wake up quietly and the sun is rising slowly. The wildlife is stirring, birds are singing. You slowly wake up too and find yourself surrounded by love and deep friendships in your teenage life. You are a perfect child.'

Nadia yawned and stretched on the couch.

'How do you feel in this moment, as you wake up in your bed, Nadia?'

'Tired, and below my belly feels funny.'

'Are you in pain?'

'No, not real pain. I can't really describe it. Just uncomfortable, kind of full or something.'

'Are you still excited about being fourteen?'

'Yeah.'

'Good. It's a special age. Please listen very carefully, young lady, for I am about to tell you something of great importance that will help you overcome this uncomfortable experience. Do you think you are mature enough to follow my instructions?'

'Uh-huh.'

'From this time onwards you must accept that you have done nothing wrong and there is no shame in your activities or thoughts during these types of experiences or others. Do you understand, Nadia?'

'Do you mean even with sex stuff too?'

'Yes, precisely, nothing to be ashamed of.'

'Nothing?'

'Absolutely nothing! Get it?'

'Uh-huh.'

'Please think about that for a moment. When you are ready, let me in on your thoughts.'

'But what about –'

'Nothing!' I severed her doubt sharply. 'Not one single thing! Having an experience is not a sin. You are a blameless child who grows into a blameless woman. Nothing to feel ashamed about. Nothing.'

Nadia's face lit up. She remained quiet whilst her mind explored the possibilities of a blameless cycle of events over which she had little control.

'I did nothing wrong!' little Nadia suddenly revealed to Ms Cape. 'It's not my fault or yours!'

'You are an intelligent, beautiful, and resourceful young lady; however, now you have matured into a woman of striking beauty and great self worth. Imagine how you look one year from today. Your hair is long and healthy and your mind is clear and focussed. Imagine no longer having the desire to punish yourself. You are blameless, but you must believe it wholeheartedly within yourself just as everyone else in your life knows it to be true. There is no room in your intellect to punish Nadia over things that were not in her control. All of Nadia is blameless. I want you to visualise this woman of the future. Visualise these changes taking effect immediately because you have self-respect now. Visualise deeply how you will present yourself confidently when you walk along the city streets today.'

Nadia viewed every frame and burned it into her life's future. She was crunching the data and keeping a permanent record as a backup file. Hopefully, there wouldn't be another crash. Nadia confirmed her resolve verbally and repeated several affirmations before I brought her back slowly.

Some patients remember the entire ordeal under a hypnotic state whilst others recall very little or nothing at all. I was yet to determine how successful this session went.

'I will count backwards from eight. You will regain your alert state and be calm and settled. Eight … seven … six … you are slowly returning. Five … four … three … you are feeling your bodily functions and moving your fingers and toes. Two … your body is feeling the natural sensations of life. One … Open your eyes slowly and be happy to be alive.'

Nadia regained her bearings and focussed her attention on Bliss for some time. 'You are very pretty,' she said.

'Thank you,' Bliss replied, a little taken aback. 'How do you feel, Nadia?'

'Oddly relaxed.'

'Just take a moment,' Bliss suggested. 'There's bottled water by your side.'

Nadia shifted position and sat upright before unscrewing the bottle cap. She took a steady sip.

'Do you have any questions, Nadia?' I asked.

'No. I don't think so; not at the moment,' she replied calmly.

'How do you see yourself in a year from now, Nadia?' I asked.

'Healthy in every way.' She looked Bliss up and down in a gesture of respect. 'Like you do. I love your hair.'

'Well, you're radiant, Nadia,' Bliss responded.

'If you have any need to see me or Bliss in the future, please contact our office and we'll make arrangements as soon as possible for you.'

'Thank you, I appreciate that.'

Bliss escorted our latest client back to the reception area, and I opened the block-out blinds of the office and squinted into the new day.

Bliss, who remained silent and professional throughout the hypnosis, entered the room as I searched for clouds in a clear sky. Sheltered from cosmic events in her classroom training, Bliss wasn't as accustomed to what I deem somewhat normal nowadays.

'What was all that about?' she began.

'Just being open,' I explained.

'Come on, Julian, that's rich coming from you.' Bliss raised her tonal vibration. 'You are the most closed-off individual I've ever met. You nearly had a psychotic episode yourself last month so please stop playing games with me.'

I turned towards my colleague with respect. 'Nadia's case is not all that uncommon.' I dropped my eyes, as if I was responsible somehow.

'Okay, I'm listening. Keep talking.'

'I have had many long-suffering people express similar experiences, even when I was on the streets trying to convert the homeless in the old system. Instead of power sockets, they will remember a huge fly on the wall or sometimes a lizard creature. That sort of thing.'

Bliss wore my comments well and searched for conviction on my face when I lifted it from the floor to look at her once more.

'I truly have no idea where our work will take us, Bliss, but I'm glad you're on this road with me.'

'At least you seemed to be going in the right direction today, despite pushing that poor woman to the edge of her sanity after you promised her you'd bring her back if she experiences discomfort.'

Her remark set off palpitations in my chest. My heart could have been in the wrong place. Direction frightens me because it could be a wrong turn based on my emotions, not that of the patient. It seems progress can only come through a fantasy world consisting of a dual perception reality. I have no compass and I feel like an inadequate pilot. If not for Bliss lighting the runway, I might not land safely these days. I often get confused between flying and falling.

'You have universal penetration that surpasses mine, Bliss,' I expressed openly. 'Yet it remains untapped due to childish reasoning. Maybe it's time to step up and polish those abilities?'

The angelic-like creature stared at me, and I felt her fighting my words; so I used stronger ones.

'Accept this; you are gifted enough to lose your mind too and reclaim the origins of your fundamental nature,' I offered.

'What are you saying?'

'There is a human condition I call "the cocoon" and I'm trying to encourage you to escape from its smothering encasing. Caterpillars belong in cocoons, butterflies belong in rainbows. You are the beautiful thing people search for when things are bleak.'

My comments needed no response, and Bliss didn't offer one. I pushed no more. She smiled as if today was the beginning of a new relationship. I turned to face the sky once again, and Bliss stood next to me looking out.

'There are clouds forming,' she said. 'Maybe your rainbow will appear soon, and you will see more than just butterflies pretending to be caterpillars, Julian.'

16

the Bible vs God

Conflict: my world is full of it and there is little escape.

As established, I once worked within the Seven Safe Religions. It was a time of great suffocation and self deprivation; of pious laws created by dead prophets and politicians. These days, as a student of the mind, I see how good intentions and prayers can simply be a symbol of greed and power.

There are dangerous people in our society who place themselves above others and recruit followers. These teachers pretend to have the knowledge and ability to fix people; to direct them to a higher level of importance. These entrepreneurs of self-help and holistic development build platforms, and the vulnerable flock to them for elevation.

Regression therapy is becoming popular again, and those who use this dangerous technique might find themselves having psychotic episodes due to unskilled practices. I often find terrified souls scratching at my door after the euphoric short-term effects of quasi therapists fail. Our truth is not worth discovering in a master's leadership camp.

Despite my reluctance to believe in any firm teachings, psychology has its merits. The term 'trigger' refers to something seen, tasted, smelt, heard, and so forth, which activates an emotional or physical response, such as severe depression or angina. The 'anchor' is the underlying culprit weighing the individual down in such situations. An anchor could drag along a sandy bottom for extended periods without getting snagged, or it could strike a reef and instantly pin down a situation.

I was drifting for many years and left it up to God and my faith to keep me from getting stranded by the nature of things. Then my life simply stopped and I became the observer. I watched the storms come and go and the tides turn, and the attitudes of people change. I was no longer Noah, and there was no flood or a civilisation to save. There was just me, and I began to notice you. Our chains have meshed together and it seems we are all stranded one way or another.

There is a thought amongst fishermen, therefore, I will cast my net and reveal my catch to you – Jesus was no fisherman. He was one of the rare fish in a vast ocean of diversity. Man made him exceptional because it is man who is so ordinary.

To find personal resolve within my environment, I swam to the shores of reason and dug out all kinds of artefacts from a fractured society. I found Jesus carved in stone, but others, not he, etched the stone. He never signed his name to it. His dreams are lost. They are dead because the churches scooped them up in holy nets and fabricated new versions of truth based on their agendas.

As for me, who am I this time? The same loner; the same intellectual; the same crazy cyclops who constantly self-diagnoses to ensure he is who I say he is. I lack common sense, but capture things beyond the reach of others. I will self-destruct at the end of my small part in society's shift of consciousness; I can feel life pressing against my nerves daily and I see the shadows searching for sunlight in the gloom.

The sun rose in an easterly direction this morning, as it always does. How bizarre. Today was destined to be a marked day in history. I sensed the importance when I woke at 4am and began writing again. My words related to a curious individual I spoke with during my sleep who would later be present in my fleshy world. I stepped out of my office when it happened, and even though I don't believe in predictions, the evidence is here in front of me now.

I approached him. I don't know why. I stood in front of him on a busy pavement in silence. Still, I don't know why. Did he look familiar to me? I don't recall noticing any of his physical features.

'We've met before, haven't we?' I asked.

'Likely, if we take into account the six degrees of separation theory.' His voice was like rusty musical notes that had a dissonant ambience.

'No, this is more than accidental interaction,' I replied. He shifted thirty-six degrees to prove a point.

'Do you believe there is a reason behind this encounter?' he proposed.

I grinned and clenched my teeth as I tried to recall something which had escaped me momentarily.

'This belongs to you.' Suddenly a folded scrap of paper sat deeply in my top pocket. 'You have a job to do. Don't let your weaknesses stop you from completing it.'

The thick crowd moved him along while my fingers dug into my shirt and retrieved the folded inscription.

Signature Post Boxes: 3S – N3 A1 T5 A2 S4

Within a few minutes by taxi, I arrived at the private PO Box address in a city backstreet. I keyed in the code at mailbox 3S, old-school style, and the metal door popped open. A collection of aging

A4 size papers filled the small compartment in an untidy bundle with discoloured and cracked rubber bands keeping them in some form of alignment. The elastics snapped the moment I placed my hand on the pile. I was running late for an important engagement, yet couldn't help but ogle the contents with a curious excitement as my cab waited.

In my possession I had printed material tightly placed against my chest and sheltered from sunlight and onlookers. Did I place these notes there years earlier because I was living a double life? Or did G put them there to fuck with me from his grave? All I can tell you is that on the journey back to Cathedral I tried answering these same questions and couldn't determine an outcome.

By convenience or coincidence, I was catching up with a former associate of the Seven Safe Religions in the afternoon. In simple terms, Father Keith Rhode is a new breed of cloth who hopes to marry the old religious covenant with the new system of spiritual freedom – a new religious squad of sorts. This old colleague is also a patient, which is probably not a good thing. Today he was doing the rounds in my area and wanted to drop in.

Irrespective of his motives, there was a personal side to our meet up. Keith is an old friend dragging a burdensome event throughout his lost years. It's my duty to help him recover his anchor so he can sail without further restrictions, but so far this rescue mission has been in turbulent weather conditions.

Religion and politics are highly volatile conversation starters. Our mild greeting swiftly shifted into a strong egoic exchange.

'How do you begin to find God if you cannot even find yourself, Keith?' I cracked. 'God is not in crisis and does not need your help.'

Keith fired back. Something about me turning to science because I couldn't handle the responsibility of truth, and another thing about the 144 000 and the end times. It was a mosh pit of desperation and I dared to stomp on old ground again.

'I work things out in my field of science when nothing else is available to me,' I said. 'Can you handle my views, or is it too much for you, Keith?'

'If it's that important to you then let's hear your instruction, but everything you ever need is in one complete book.' Keith raised his finger and shook it at me. 'You should have stuck to your original calling, Julian.'

'Your opinion belongs to you, which is fine.' I eased off a little. 'The Bible is the best-selling works of all time and yet its authors are many. Keith, in my world of problem solving I simply pose questions until the questions themselves inevitably turn into sound answers. Even when no evidence to my questions exist.'

'That sounds contrived,' he said. 'How could a question be anything other than a question?'

'My logic is that many of the questions cancel each other out by simple reasoning. Keith, do you mind if I ask you a series of questions to elaborate?'

'Go ahead.'

'Okay, here we go. Question one: How do we know the Bible is entirely true?'

'Because it is God's Word.'

'Question two: Who wrote the Bible?'

'God.'

'Question three: How did God write the Bible?'

'He used men.'

'Back to Question one: How do we know the Bible is entirely true?'

'Because God used men to write it down under a kind of trance.'

'Question four: Does God lie?'

'No.'

'Question five: Does God make mistakes?'

'Of course not.'

'Question six: Is the entire Bible God's work?'

'Yes.'

Keith scratched his head and moved uncomfortably in his chair.

'Let me ask you question one again: How do we know that the Bible is entirely true?'

'Because the Bible writers clearly declared this to be so.'

'Question seven: Does God know Earth is a sphere and not flat?'

'Of course.'

'Again I ask you: Does God make mistakes?'

'And again I tell you, of course not! Where are you going with this line of questioning?'

'Question eight: Do men make mistakes?'

'Yes, you know they do!'

'Question one again: How do we know the Bible is true?'

'Because the Bible says so.'

'Question seven again: Does God know Earth is a sphere and not flat?'

'Of course!'

'Question nine: Why does the Bible suggest numerous times that Earth is flat?'

'Because men make mistakes, not God!'

'Question one again: How do we know the Bible is entirely true?'

'Because God used these men to write it.'

I kept silent. The mental exercise was over, and Father Keith absorbed what was said before I continued.

'You said, "men make mistakes", Keith. Men wrote the Bible and perhaps they believed they were doing God's work,' I suggested. 'The fact is, humans make human errors. Yet this is impossible according to religious zealots because God was in control of the scribes and the only thing written was truth. And so the loop continues. My simple questions reveal mistakes were made, and given that God does not lie or make mistakes, we can easily conclude that the scribes thought God was using them to do His work. Isn't that the essence of all cults, a sense of doing God's work?'

'Brother Julian, I have no time for mind games and inconsequential party tricks,' Keith said. 'I take my work seriously.'

'Yes, I'm sure you do, and so do I, Keith. You have to remember that I have been on both sides of the fence and I can assure you the grass is patchy everywhere.'

'Well, what do you suggest then?'

'Destroying the fence and all other barriers, maybe even face your –'

'I have to go now,' Father Keith interrupted. 'Thank you for your time today. Goodbye.'

'I understand. Before you disappear, please take this with you.'

'Take what, Julian?'

'A paralysing fear of death,' I said cryptically.

'I beg your pardon?'

'Peculiar, isn't it?'

'Isn't what peculiar, Julian?'

'You have this condition – a paralysing fear of death – and yet you try to convince yourself otherwise by burying it with Scriptures tainted with terror.' Keith was halfway through the door when he heard these closing words. 'You need to die a little to receive appreciation and growth.'

Losing friends is an occupational hazard. I sensed I had just lost my last from the old system.

With my scheduled social appointment over after it had barely begun, I retrieved the bundle of papers from my locked draw and inspected its contents. A newfound friend hugged me. The documents appeared to be an anthology of personal observations and interviews conducted by a woman by the name of Ravine Arcane. My guess is it's not her real name due to an obvious play on words.

It was a struggle to put these notes away before my next patient arrived. Tiffany was born a male and decided that being female was more in line with her identity. I, along with Father Keith, had once policed the religious law and pushed such individuals aside. I am grateful for Tiffany's trust in me now, after my other life refused to see her as an equal human being in our society.

These days, I'm proud of my spiritual whoredom. The pleasure of bondage can only get us so far before the pleasure is lost and true pain is felt. Yes, I do see highly religious people as sex addicts looking for that next orgasm – that next hallelujah!

17

1964 and the beast

I want to show you something that is hidden. Come twist your faith, just a little. Come fracture your mind and let it heal in its own time. Play with fire and watch it burn the hedge down so we can see your neighbours more clearly. I am going to exercise the dog called Possession in your backyard.

We live in a world where there are pills for possession. There are medications to lessen the pain and suffering that demons inflict on the sick of mind. Attachment of beasts – creatures with no faces – live like parasites on hosts and suck them dry of spiritual strength. Ravine Arcane entered my world with a powerful bug spray and cleaning agents.

I shuffled through her work and noticed they appeared to be of historical value, and much like my life, the pages are randomly placed in a nonlinear fashion. Like a young child at a school carnival, I turned my head away and gently slipped my fingers in the lucky dip and picked a winner. The heading on the page simply read: 1964.

1964 is the number of the Beast, isn't it? Maybe it ought to be, for that was the year the Order of the Exorcist was detached from the Church. That was the year the Second Vatican Council included Satan in talks by ignoring that he has any power at all. In that year of 1964, the art of exorcism within the Roman Catholic Church ceased to operate in the new rite of priestly ordination.

The year I write in is unimportant, for the book of life always identifies chapters using emotional connections, not numbers. Bookmarks only represent shifts in global consciousness.

Rome wasn't built in a day, as many like to over-phrase, for the city continues to take shape after the first stone was positioned. Many of its laws have silently passed away along with those individuals who once followed them. A highly religious friend once told me how possession is a gradual illness.

'You cannot suddenly catch it,' she said. 'You only need to forget Satan, or ignore evil, to be infected by his power!'

This friend I speak of is seriously careful not to allow demons enter her life. She has a crucifix at the ready in one hand and beads in the other. The Bible is close to her heart, and she has learnt every relevant quote to debate Satan and my questions. It seems she has already caught the disease: a life of great suffering. The devil has taken over her life and she believes the opposite.

Despite my attitude towards regimented protocol, I'd do anything to bring people closer together. Therein sits my passion. I find it tragic that God affects them all and they become obsessed with the things they detest, rather than things bringing them pure joy.

My friend says, 'There is only one Evil, but the faceless enemy masquerades as many and infects all who allow it to enter.'

The exorcist knows when a possessed individual is fully handed over to the one called Lucifer. Interestingly, Lucifer is also known as the *light-bringing morning star; technically the planet Venus when appearing as the morning star.*

The victims of possession are usually of some strong religious background, baptised or christened in the name of Jesus and exorcised in the name of Christ. There appears to be a connection and a major flaw.

Yes, the year is unimportant; however, there is a shift in global consciousness taking place. The Globally Ordained Division is gaining power and they will use 'possession' as an excuse to exercise their self-serving agenda. This bookmark in time will change the course of history, and the guards.

Here, in this instance, I will introduce you to the devil I know today, the same devil that always was. Created by man in order to put a financial price on fear. The root of all evil is our reluctance to recognise our own ignorance.

I put the page down and looked at the time displayed on my desktop computer and noted the current date. I stared at it until the numbers become one soft image in my eyes. Time itself is only relevant for growth during the here and now; beyond physical death it becomes irrelevant once more. My automatic responses eventually made my eyelids blink and I came back to the moment. How did I feel? Like an animal of God who bit Satan's hand and tasted human blood and flesh. I felt as though Hell had no boundaries and I didn't need a key to enter Heaven. I felt purpose. I realised there was nothing sudden in my decision to turn my back on the priesthood. It was always following me.

I accept that religion is not about the individual, it's about numbers, and, like a confused moth, the individual followed two lights. One is man, the other is something still unknown but always close by.

It bothers me to watch people repeatedly smack their heads against a wailing wall or kiss the ground. Maybe it's more of a participation sport? The muffles of a priest in a large room are particularly torturous, especially when one word swallows another.

I find a friend in my emotional drinking and self-absorbed philosophical memoirs, as you can plainly see. I cannot discover joy in pure fictional literature because I find it difficult to get excited about something created out of a challenge, rather than driven from actual experiences. This could be the reason why I struggled at Sunday School. With the stinging warmth of unmolested alcohol trickling down my throat, I hit the pages again and found an entry labeled 'Cloned'.

In our world, cloning and its implications attracts strong ethical debates and emotional reactions. Dolly the cloned sheep and South Korea's dog, Snoopy, have triggered heated discussions around the world. More often than not, people from a variety of faiths find the concept of laboratory creation insulting.

Regardless of some ethical considerations, medical scientists find elements of this subject matter appealing and potentially beneficial for humankind. Similar to other moral debates, such as abortion, cloning is a hot topic with undefined edges. Nevertheless, let us obtain facts before throwing away the elements of good along with the freakish. Cells regenerate naturally, and many medical achievements resulted from cloning technology. Surgeons have been cultivating skin for years and help many burns sufferers in the process. It was not long ago when certain religions forbade organ transplants because they believed a new soul would occupy the recipient's body and personality. A blood transfusion would have had similar results too according to their creed.

Even Superman could not fight the farce of a dud generation of political leaders who refused to push ahead in life-saving stem cell applications. As of writing, Germany is one of the leaders in this type of cell technology with a reputation to literally mend damaged hearts. Using a method in which stem cells are extracted from bone marrow (usually from the hip area) the regenerating cells are injected into the heart where they bring life back to dead sections of the vital organ. This relatively simple procedure has prolonged countless lives and saved much grief and medical expense compared to traditional less effective techniques, such as heart transplants. The quality of life a patient experiences is dramatically improved and progressively optimised as nature intended it. This is the verdict so far and the zombie apocalypse has not happened yet.

Many countries have now standardised the procedure of retaining stem cells from every newborn's umbilical cord for that child's future, lest he or she should need unforeseen medical treatment. The most dogmatic individuals who reject this technology might soften their stance if they held their own child after lifesaving treatment was performed. Perhaps they would praise God for such scientific miracles when they sense a soul still exists when illness has disappeared.

The Raëlians, an alien-belief movement synonymous with pro cloning, believe we are the creation of an alien race – not a single God, but many gods (Elohim). Whether seemingly intelligent folks are drawn to such organisations because of sincere faith, lifestyle, controversy, or boredom, is not fully understood by those standing on the outside looking in. Many famous movie stars have joined the ranks of other hardcore movements who pin their continual success on fundamentalism. It is easy to conclude that many of us need a central belief system, even if it wobbles our logic at times and goes against the grain of public direction.

I pushed aside this intriguing entry to reach for another whilst spinning my drink in a small glass. I already know the outcome of the

Raëlian Movement and the Clonaid saga. I live in an age where tightly controlled monitoring of stem cell research and other quasi-sinful developments are commonplace. There are no Frankenstein laboratories, just preservation and cultivation of living cells, usually from the same recipient. This measure is to save lives, not to create them. Fewer debilitating illnesses, such as Parkinson's disease, Alzheimer's disease and organ failures, are the result of such initiatives. Wheelchair usage for spinal cord injuries is usually a temporary vehicle between medical procedures these days. Neuro technology is also alive and well. Paraplegics can now move limbs using thoughts transmitted by sensors attached to the brain. Amputees make use of artificial limbs using a similar process. In some regards we are stepping out of the primitive age.

The next page in my hand contained one part of an interview that appeared to be of religious origin. All was not what it seemed at first glance though. Interviews with priests don't often highlight extraterrestrial-based themes and other elements of disclosure. I scrambled for the accompanying pages and found what appeared to be the beginning of the related chapter. This material excited me on a personal level and it will find a way into my own work in progress, Bleedthrough, which in turn is finding its way into your personal framework of reality.

What led me to this treasure trove of Ravine Arcane's work synonymous with my style of writing? Was G really homeless? Was he even real? Where was my headspace? Was it really a question of me and my identity at the time; the peeling away of my own mask? I cannot stop. I pick up another section, another organ, and try and place it into my broken life.

18

unbelievable

I found Julian slumped over his desk the following morning. He was wearing the same clothes and clutching a half-empty scotch bottle. The clinic was perfumed with man odour and hard liquor. His face was planted in a pile of papers, which I later discovered to be Ravine's work. This was not the first time I found him in this condition, but it would be the last if I had anything to do with it. We had a patient arriving in half an hour so I gently nudged Julian until he woke. He rolled his red eyes up at me and lifted his head slightly. A piece of paper was sticking to his cheek. I grabbed his bottle, closed the cap tight and pulled him into the moment. I keep an aromatherapy spritz handy at all times, which I sprayed around the room much to his protest. Eventually, he dragged to his feet and began to align his bearings for the psychiatry session ahead. He proceeded to slowly stack Ravine's papers.

'Leave it', I told him. 'I'll sort it and put them in your desk.'

Julian went to freshen up, and I asked our receptionist if she could bring a coffee and a few pastries whilst I wiped down the benches and tidied up a bit. When Julian returned he entered the room with a coffee in one hand and a custard tart in the other, dropping crumbs everywhere. The first thing he said was, 'Where are the papers?'. After a short discussion I reminded him about our first patient, Emily Hopkins. I have noticed that Julian's short-term memory is slipping a bit lately, but he seemed to recall the details of this case quite distinctly.

I began a somewhat sketchy session without the presence of Bliss Stone.

'Poltergeist,' a young mother revealed during the consultation. 'It has turned my world upside-down.'

'Please tell me all you can, Emily,' I encouraged, despite having the referral fresh in my mind.

'Always the same, I wake up in the dead of night and feel this thing sitting on my chest, choking me with unseen hands. The stranglehold goes on for a few minutes until I almost pass out. Then the ghost, or whatever the hell it is, retreats.'

'You never pass out?' I asked.

'No. As if the thing knows when to stop so it can torment me well after it has gone,' she said. 'Things get moved around too. Toys switch themselves on and lights flicker. You probably think I'm a crackpot, don't you? Just like all the other doctors.'

I remained quiet. Something about that word 'crackpot' kept me from speaking. I briefly revisited my early childhood where I was accused of being a 'nutter' after I told some friends I had been held against my will by an older kid and his adult siblings. It was a strange set of circumstances that saw me tied up in a stranger's housing commission yard and threatened with petrol and fire. Some things just never leave me. It was being unheard that hurt the most.

'Hey!' Emily brought me back to the moment. 'I know this is a nuthouse, but I'm really not crazy. I just need tactics to deal with these experiences.'

'I take my patients seriously, Emily, and your wellbeing is my first priority,' I explained. 'I was informed that you refuse to take medication, which might help you relax during these encounters?'

'Yeah, I'm strongly against any form of drugs and unfortunately homeopathic treatments aren't working for me at the moment,' she admitted.

'Medication is not for everyone,' I said. 'It is a choice, but you're obviously distressed and we need to find some kind of treatment that will help you function.'

'Do you believe these experiences I'm having are real or in my head?' Emily was clearly testing me after getting nowhere fast with other therapists.

'Based on the information you have given me, I know you are experiencing some kind of real trauma. I have no doubts about that.' I wanted to build a foundation of trust.

'It is real all right! Just look at my hands, trembling just from the thought of it.'

'Have you tried changing rooms, Emily?'

'Yes. I even moved house three times, all for nothing.'

'There is obviously an attachment, don't you think?' I began to lead my patient down another corridor of thought.

'What do you mean by that, doctor?'

'You have a child, don't you?' I asked knowingly.

'Yes, but she is only five years old and doesn't appear to be affected in any way by the poltergeist activity,' Emily answered assertively. 'Why is that relevant?'

It was not my intention to answer Mrs Hopkins' question because it was all part of the treatment process I had planned with my colleague. Bliss walked into the therapy session at the appropriate moment. She had been observing the proceedings from her adjacent office and waited for the cue.

'Sorry, Professor, I didn't realise you were with someone,' she apologised.

I directed my attention back to my patient. 'I am terribly sorry for the interruption, Mrs Hopkins. You will have to forgive my colleague, we share the same office space sometimes and –'

'No, no, it's okay, really.'

'That's very kind of you, Mrs Hopkins,' Bliss replied before diverting her attention elsewhere in the room. 'And what's your name, little man?' she asked an empty chair. 'You're such a cutie.'

My patient and I looked at one another in a confused state. Our concerns were then redirected towards Bliss.

'Bliss, who are you talking to?' I asked gingerly.

'The young boy. Your son, Mrs Hopkins?' The question was squarely directed at the stunned patient.

'The good lady does not have a son,' I said. 'Let's talk later. Okay?'

'Bobby?' escaped through the patient's lips. 'Bobby!'

'Bliss, could you please give us a moment?' I asked.

'Certainly,' she replied with a raised eyebrow and slipped out of the consultation quietly.

'At your own pace, Emily,' I said gently. 'Does this mean something to you? Does it have any significance to your experiences?'

'Yes.' She rocked back and forth, sobbing with joy and heartache. 'It all makes sense now.'

'What makes sense?' I asked.

'Bobby is my first child,' she revealed for the first time during any psychological consultation. 'He and my husband died in a helicopter accident during a flight in Cape York when I was pregnant with my daughter.'

'Sorry to hear that, Emily. That's most tragic,' I expressed. 'Do you think, maybe…?'

'Yes. There is no poltergeist choking me. Bobby is giving me mummy hugs and kisses!'

Mrs Hopkins cried with healing tears, and I gave her plenty of time to compose herself. Eventually she spoke through a veil of tissues instead of a veil of darkness.

'He just wants to be close to me,' she explained further.

'And do you think that's why the experiences continued no matter where you relocated to?' I loaded the final bullet in an attempt to kill her poltergeist once and for all.

'Yes, my boy just wants to be with his mum.'

'Therefore you are not really being choked?' I continued with the theme. 'You are perhaps holding your breath subconsciously and gagging with unexplained emotions?'

'I know that's how it is,' she accepted.

Mrs Hopkins was given forty minutes on the couch, and Bliss quietly watched and listened from another room. I helped my patient visualise strategies to deal with any further episodes should they arise. Emily saw her deceased son as a guardian angel of sorts who would grow as she does spiritually. I suggested in hypnotherapy that Bobby still relied on his mother to nurture him by example. Hopefully, this will motivate Emily to continue her journey in life and tackle the many years ahead in a more positive way. At the very least, she might find comfort in the uncomfortable and unavoidable.

'Would you like me to organise further counselling to help you deal with your situation, Emily?'

'No thanks, I have my boy back. Everything is as good as it can be. Your colleague is something else, isn't she?'

'Bliss? She is definitely a unique individual,' I agreed.

'Please thank her for me.'

Bliss expressed strong disapproval of any involvement in this setup until I asked her for alternatives. This woman, Emily, had reached the end of the path, like so many others we catch in the system. We, our little clinic in Cathedral, could be the last stop for people who would otherwise keep walking until they fall off the radar permanently. I have lost some patients to suicide, and I no longer give a fuck about legal obligations, bureaucratic or ethical bullshit. I hope Bliss will come to see why we regularly need to arm ourselves with creativity in order to set people free. It does sit heavily on my shoulders and in my heart that our professional environment sometimes turns into a masquerade party. Then again, life is one big pretend and we all wear disguises.

Masks were omnipresent in Ravine Arcane's writings. This is precisely what lured me back to her pages that night, despite my exhaustion.

19

Catholics on the line

Ravine Arcane writes:

My day job as a journalist takes me to many remote locations and extremely tight cities. Regardless of landscape, population, politics, or cultural divides, my most challenging assignments have involved inaccessibility of the mind.

Some women call me a role model for aspiring females, but I prefer not to get into the gender debate because being a woman has nothing to do with being a role model. In fact, highlighting one gender over another could lead to further segregation. Regardless of my gender or yours, our inspiration should come from passion, not physical or emotional orientation. Not one woman can speak on behalf of another women, because we all have driving factors separating us. Many of us have a psychological edge over the men in our lives; unfortunately, some of us were simply raised to believe otherwise. It's true many women are entering domains traditionally marked by men. Females now have high-level roles in science, politics, and religion. However, public approvals of these establishments are changing.

Last week, a local radio station announced in their 9am news bulletin how a survey revealed people nowadays have less confidence in politicians and churches, but have greater confidence in medicines and science. I recall this vividly because I was literally reaching for painkillers at the time to ease my period discomfort. The churches have been under a lot of media heat lately due to various things, such as child abuse and cruel psychological practices that extract money from patrons. I wasn't interested in crashing into that roadblock because there was something else I wanted to explore.

My first action was to contact a national church at random by phone. The following is what happened with all the names and locations changed:

'Good morning. Sister Marilyn speaking. How may I help you?'

'Hello Sister, my name is Ravine Arcane. I'm in the process of conducting some research about belief systems, and I would like to talk to someone about UFOs and extraterrestrials.'

'O' good Lord!'

'Yes, I appreciate it sounds a bit strange, but I'm keen to speak with someone who might be open to this discussion. You see, I'm trying to research people's beliefs and understand how, if they do at all, tie in with the church and its views.'

'Oh? I see.'

'I know very little about the Catholic Church's point of view on this subject. Could you give me any of your personal thoughts about this, as a starting point for further discussion perhaps?'

'Jesus came to save us. That's all we knew at the time and continue to observe today.'

'So what do you believe regarding the UFO phenomenon?'

'Well, it's only my view and not necessarily that of the Catholic Church, but aliens could be real. It's simply unknown to us at this time;

but if it's that important, then God would certainly reveal it to us when the time is right.'

The elderly sounding lady surprised me with her manner. I don't know why I was expecting a rigid personality on the line; one who would simply cut that question down rather than give it some consideration.

'Would you see UFOs as a threat if you saw one? Or would you lean towards something more angelic, Sister?'

'We don't have a strong anti-Satan tradition in our current Church. Yes, I know it was a totally different situation in the old tradition.'

I learnt something right away from this woman and I felt at odds with my perceptions. Maybe the media, my own people, had me caught up in stereotyping to the point that it affected my judgement. I had always imagined the Catholic Church of being dogmatic and using tradition at their disposal when questioned or tested. This is, however, early days in my research. As Sister Marilyn suggested, it was only her opinion, a personal one with a connection to religious teachings.

I wanted to get back on the ET topic, so I asked her about the possibilities of other life forms again. Judging by her response, I deducted that she was somewhat of a believer in such vague matters and gave me a good narrative to demonstrate this point.

'When we consider that 600 years ago the fence was around everyone in Europe, and people believed nothing existed outside of Europe except the edge of a flat world, we cannot simply dismiss any possibilities of other worlds. Look at the new lands that Marco Polo reached. And, you know, some people still believe the world is flat.'

After her line of reasoning she began to talk about the 'Rites of the Catholic Church'. She made a point of spelling 'RITES'. My pen was running out of ink like a true professional and I lost much of the dialogue. I reached for another.

'I'm sorry for my ignorance,' I said, 'but is your religion's title Catholic Church or Roman Catholic Church?'

'We certainly prefer Catholic rather than Roman Catholic.'

'Are you all under the same group?' My uncouth manner did not seem to bother the lady. In hindsight I should have used the term 'order' instead of 'group'.

'Yes, but there are many branches, even Russian Catholics.'

'I understand the Catholic Church chose to canonise other books into its Bible in the fifteen hundreds as part of the Apocrypha; would that be correct?'

'Yes, and isn't it funny how we always get people saying to us, "You don't have the entire Bible!" The irony is that we have more than other religions, more Scriptures.'

'Do some of these writings contain celestial, as in alien content?'

'Yes, but you clearly get that in other religion's Bibles, too. You don't need to look further than Ezekiel to notice this.'

'So why does your particular faith have more books, Sister?'

'With the Old Testament, the Protestants accepted only what the Jews accepted. Anything not written in Hebrew, the Jews did not canonise. Basically, we did accept some of the Apocrypha.'

Whilst we were talking, I sensed others were waiting for her assistance, so I thanked her respectfully for her insight and time. In return, she gave me the phone number for the Catholic University HQ and strongly suggested I use it.

I was polite with Sister Marilyn and she was polite with me, despite my unusual questions. I just hope the next person I speak with will be equally open to my research questions.

I continued reading the follow-up of Ravine's experiences with the church and alien concepts. According to her, the following entry was written some days later after a conversation with the mentioned

Catholic University. The receptionist put Ravine through to a representative called Father John McKenzie. The topic of discussion is the same; however, the outcome is quite different.

'Father John McKenzie here, how may I assist you?' The tone of his voice was youthful, warm and friendly.

'Hello Father, my name is Ravine Arcane. I'd like to discuss the UFO topic, particularly regarding humanoid extraterrestrials,' I explained.

'That's fascinating subject matter. Are you … umm, why do you wish to discuss this?'

'I'm trying to write a book on the subject and intend to record numerous findings from a variety of faiths. I want to examine this phenomenon, whether it's real or imaginary, to see if it somehow blends in with spirituality and biblical theology. From my perspective, it seems to be an important issue amongst many religions, but not really spoken of in their everyday teachings.'

'That's some task,' he said. Father John seemed to value my intention.

I was particularly interested what stance churches took on the subject because most traditional churches were in service hundreds of years ago, and could have structures in place to tackle such enquiries.

I spoke on the phone with Father John for some time about the topic, but at first there was a lot of generalisation. He went on to speak about stigmata, Mother Mary's weeping statues, and apparitions with nothing being confirmed or denied. Father John suggested I visit the Vatican's website and also the Catechism of the Catholic Church website for further directions. This would guide me to 'official' beliefs. The dedicated patron explained that searching for words such as 'aliens' and 'UFOs' would probably not produce results and I would have to use other variations to get the right information. He might have known this from personal experience.

During the next few minutes, Father John again raised the issue of what an interesting topic extraterrestrials posed, yet stopped short of expressing any solid beliefs of his own. I'm unsure if this was due to personal choice or a religiously motivated resistance to speak out. I waited for a change, but it never came.

I thanked him for his time. He jotted down my email address in case he found other information to pass on. There was, however, more that needed to be said. Moments before hanging up, Father John made the following important statement, which could easily explain his reluctance to commit to a certain view.

'Churches differ on views even at the most senior levels – not officially, only in private. They – Church patrons – might believe in such things – as alien encounters – regardless of the Church's official stance.'

Shortly after our conversation ended, I followed Father John's suggestions and inputted the recommended names into a search engine. Just as he had predicted, finding relevant information was near impossible. In fact, I became so frustrated that I decided to leave the Catholics to their private thoughts, at least for the time being.

Ravine Arcane's notes would further highlight her failed attempts at gaining information from UFO interest groups too. She'd left numerous unanswered messages in many centres, which frustrated her to no end. If Ravine's work became published, these groups could express their beliefs and experiences to a wider community; but, I guess they didn't care much for that kind of publicity.

As I continued to slide my way through Ravine's other entries, I noticed she couldn't let the Catholic views, or lack of them, rest. The Catholic Church was one of the most influential institutions on the planet in those days; therefore, Ravine found it difficult to believe they would be unable to offer some form of further insight on extraterrestrial matters.

Individuals, such as myself, can easily agree that the Roman Catholic Church had a history of keeping a firm stance on many topics over the centuries, such as abortion and homosexuality. Their influence continued into my generation as part of the Seven Safe Religions. Even Ravine Arcane commented it was a big deal when the Pope finally accepted that condoms were a lesser evil than AIDS.

I am beside myself yet again. I feel whole. These words confirm I was not alone in my independent thoughts during my churchy years, despite my external actions. The world and I spin in different orbits, which becomes a temporary comfort for my vertigo. Like fish bones in a dried-up lakebed, it should have been foreseen that these bones would fossilise one day and rise to the surface once more.

Extraterrestrials have not revealed themselves to the populace, despite heavy suggestions they would. In the manner of Jesus Christ's return, our heavenly hosts were said to arrive when we least expect them. The alien connection did find an audience though, and it resulted in new reinterpretations of many Holy Books.

A new Bible for a new belief system – it's an old idea that works time and time again. 'Old Light' and 'New Light', by which the Jehovah's Witnesses used to govern until that dim light became blindingly obvious. The same God, different shit.

I know there will be little sleep tonight. I'm impulsive when a good story comes along. Unfortunately, time doesn't permit me to take on the huge task alone. With all other priorities squeezing me out of existence, the only person I can trust with all my notes is Bliss Stone. I hope she is willing to participate.

20

inside out

The last time Father Keith visited Julian at our clinic it ended with a war of words. Honestly, I felt horrified when I read the account in his journal. Such an exchange should not take place within our professional environment.

Father Keith's most recent appointment came out of necessity – he had a desperate and sensitive need to seek help from us. Being a priest had its fair share of secrets, and it seemed Keith had some deep-seated ones. I felt a little uneasy about this purely clinical visit because Julian suspected the outcome of this session would be extremely confronting for the black and white thinker. It began civilly, professionally, and ended with a most dramatic revelation that taught me a thing or two about human thresholds.

'Thanks for seeing me on such short notice, Brother Julian. I hope there are no hard feelings between us.'

'Not from where I'm standing, Keith,' I affirmed. I reached out and offered my hand. He took a step forward and gave me a half embrace. 'Look, I understand you're here for a reason and not just circular chit chat, so why don't we just get straight into it and give you the peace of mind you deserve.'

'Straight to the couch then?' he replied with a nervous smile.

'Take your shoes off and make yourself comfortable,' I said. My friendship with Keith was already strained and I had to be mindful to keep the trust well and truly alive before the session stepped into the subconscious. I was extra polite, extra personable, and did not speak of any politics. I had not touched a drop of alcohol for a couple of days and was very committed to delivering an outcome. 'I normally have my colleague, Bliss, present when performing these hypnotic sessions. Would it bother you if she joins us?'

'No, not at all, let the lass be part of this experience too,' he said.

Bliss did not have any scheduled appointments due to a client's medical cancellation, so I invited her to the show. She sat quietly like a still-life model. Keith settled and closed his eyes, giving full attention to the procedure at hand.

I began voice direction. I processed whether I'd get another chance to help Keith with his underlying issues, so I flew as quick as possible all the way to that place he didn't want to revisit or reveal. I had touched this huge wall in other sessions, but could not scale it. The following account is generalised and compressed from an extraordinarily long and intense sitting.

Irrespective of my initial concerns, Keith managed to reproduce experiences during his preadolescence. My direction led to happy moments. These were stereotypical events such as camping trips and Christmas get-togethers. Progressing throughout the years, we tried to find that weak link in a strong chain that had caused him so much tension with interpersonal relationships. I knew it was somewhere because I saw physical signs of it in his mannerisms. We ran into an issue of trust, again. Keith was not progressing and circled crucial events like a dragon ready for a fiery attack. My determination was stronger and Keith's wall gradually crumbled. I began stepping through the rubble of old ruins.

'You are both the observer and the experiencer now, Keith. I want you to go back to the time when Keith Rhode was involved in a railway train disaster. You are this young teenager, but today you are also going to place yourself in the minds of your doctors and immediate family. I want you to feel and understand their emotional struggles with the tragedy. Do you understand, Keith?'

'Yes.'

'Good. Although you might feel uncomfortable and emotional, please remember you are protected, because you are an observer. No real harm will come to you. Now, please tell me, who is with Keith Rhode on the train when it derails?'

'Lance Miles.'

'Is anybody else you know onboard?'

'No.'

'Does Lance Miles survive the accident?'

'No.'

'Where is Lance Miles in relation to you after the crash?' I asked.

Keith paused for a moment and processed my question.

'Most of him is on the other side of the mangled carriage with the others.'

'Do you recognise him in this tangle of wreckage?'

'Yes. His head is in my hands.' Keith raised his arms slightly before resting them again; one of them flopped on the floor.

According to investigation reports, Keith was unable to move due to his injuries and was confined in a small space when they found him. I decided to move on and not get caught in those details for now.

'Is Lance Miles a friend of yours?' Keith was reluctant to answer and seemed a bit confused. I rephrased the question. 'Was Keith Rhode a friend of Lance Miles, and if so, in what capacity?'

'Yes. They were lovers.'

'In what capacity were Keith Rhode and Lance Miles lovers?'

'Sexually experimental.'

'Okay, good. Now we are going to go forward in time when Keith Rhode is taken to the emergency room. Again, please remember that you are Keith Rhode, but no harm will come to you during this observation of yourself and that of others around you. I want you to focus on emotions and procedures, those that stand out foremost in your mind. You are a fly on the wall and a mind reader too. Do you understand what you must do?'

'Yes.'

'Good. Now give me a detailed summary of what is going on around you and how you and others actually feel during the months and years of therapy. Speak whatever comes to mind and do not stop to analyse your observations. You will do this later in private thought. Do you understand what you must do?'

'Yes.'

'Good. Begin in the operating room. Explain it at a safe distance, but be part of the experience too. You are the narrator and the subject also. What is happening to you, Keith?'

He took a noticeably deep breath and dove straight into the blood and guts of the experience.

'The surgeons are ripping me open in places where I'm not already torn. They rearrange my organs so I don't drown in my own bodily fluids. My soul has left my body several times, and I feel no pain. The surgeons eventually win over my physical body, and I attach myself to it again. It's a heavy burden. I don't like being trapped in there, that beaten up body. I'm in critical recovery for months. Priests and nuns have been visiting me daily, reading bible teachings. I feel responsible for the sin I have committed. For the death of the people in Carriage 9. My sexual organ has been damaged, and I feel undeserving of pleasure. I'm neither here nor there; everything is odd. Some things are painful and others are numb. It hurts to think straight. I have trouble recalling my first eleven years, but the last few burn. I'm dealing with my sin by practicing self-discipline and praying heavily for salvation,' Keith explained.

'Tell me about your family, Keith. What is your relationship like with them during the physical and emotional recovery process?'

'In this very spot where I'm holding onto my walking stick, there used to stand a boy with a trademark smile, so I'm told. I wish I could be that good son once more. He means well, my dad, but he sure does have some strange ways of expressing it. "Stop dawdling and get a move on!", he hollers. Mum rolls her eyes and shakes her head at my slow progress. Can't blame them really. We're running late for our Church service because of me.'

'How does that make you feel, Keith?'

'Dirty and unworthy,' he said.

'Why do you feel dirty and unworthy, Keith?'

'Because I feel ashamed of what I've done to them?'

'And what did you do to them?'

'You know, that thing with the older kid that died. I told the priest everything at the hospital. I'm sure he told them.'

'Okay, let's get back to your parents,' I said. 'How do you feel when they tell you to hurry up?'

'I feel them suffering with the pain that should solely belong to me. After all, I caused the anger in God because I slept with another boy. When I lay unconscious, my parents were fully aware. When I was anaesthetised, they held my hand. When I was under the knife, they put their hands together in prayer. Whenever I forget, they are always remembering.'

'What about you, Keith? How do you live through this experience?'

'I force one foot in front of the other and try to push bad memories aside, but those dark shadows keep following me. There are so many things I'm unable to do. People are quick to label me as disabled in some way, which is a fair description. But what they fail to realise is that within this shell lies my fundamental nature, which is not cracked or faulty in any way. In fact, my internal reflexes are so swift my body cannot react in time. Although I cry and hardly laugh, I still remain whole inside the broken bits of me. I have worth, but people seem to ignore my voice even when I scream silently at them from the pit of my despair.'

There was silence, and I let the silence have its own voice for a while until our room was in tune with the sounds of sobbing. Keith was in his own isolation growth chamber. Bliss Stone and I sat in the parallel universe and made observations. She looked at me from across the room and questioned if this session had finished. Her eyes were darting between me and the patient. I shook my head; not just yet.

'The turmoil you face is your own, Keith,' I explained. 'It is only when you personally take responsibility for it that you will see it dissolve and become more manageable. You have done well, Keith. You do have great worth and you are recognised for it. You also have outstanding lateral thinking and are tolerant of all peaceful ideals. You are kind to yourself and your sexuality, as well as other lifestyles, without harsh judgement.

'After you repeat the following affirmations you will put them into practice ... You will slowly open your eyes as I count backwards from seven, from six, five ... four ... three ... two, one.'

Keith sat up on the couch and smiled like he meant it for the first time in years. He was not entirely aware of what intention was placed upon his soul. The seed for recovery was sown deep; therefore it might take a few seasons before it fruits.

'Is there something you would like to discuss with me, Keith?' I asked. 'A question or two?'

'No, nothing really,' he said. 'I prefer not to know what happened. I just need to trust that you gave it your best shot.'

Bliss observed our interaction and inched her way closer with an impossible silence. She knows my desire to disrupt authoritarian religions at every opportunity. I know her thoughts on my actions too, which can be quite confronting for me at times.

'It was nice meeting you, Father Keith.'

'Miss Stone.' He took a step back. 'Sorry my dear, I forgot you were present.'

'That's all right, Father. I don't mind that sometimes. Good luck with everything.'

Bliss and I debriefed after Keith left. I took the opportunity to delve deeper into her lifestyle opinions. For her, homosexuality was nothing to think twice about; however, it was considered a sin by religious standards. Bliss was spared the semantics of my, and Father Keith's, time. Her generation carved the way forward to equality and a new wave of sexual freedoms. Some days, I long for these sexual freedoms to find me.

21

touch, but don't feel

Whilst Keith reasons with the ghosts of his past, I searched for something more physical to alleviate the curse of fleshy desires. Friday nights are traditionally filled with high expectations for sexually deprived singles. Where does my introverted self belong on nights like this? I'm not entirely sure. The original Sabbath casts a cold shadow over my enthusiasm and I normally stay indoors, as if I were practising abstinence. Should I go out and find clever conversation, companionship or even love? Or should I just order online and get home delivery again?

I have already been through the five stages of a break up: denial, resentment, bargaining, depression, and acceptance, although not necessarily in that order. Okay, I still might be feeling some of those symptoms, but my work and the occasional alcoholic binge helps me mask those blemishes. I am now married to my patients and committed to their wellbeing, but that's also pushing me towards another kind of divorce.

I will reveal a secret to all the women out there. Men, no matter how 'nice' they seem or how 'professional' they appear, are visual creatures with a shallow depth of field. These inherited traits are ever-present and I desire the sense of touch to feel alive. Yes, I'm a lone wolf with primal urges, because males aged eight to eighty-eight have sexual weaknesses.

It was Friday the thirteenth – how appropriate. My mood was dismal and my compass was heading south.

Although Ravine's notes were stacked on my coffee table, my Wild Turkey ran like the Dickens with Shakespeare in my head, and I lost the passion to get through another act alone. My thoughts turned to the young women downstairs laughing. The sound of their high heels walking on concrete drew me to my window. I enjoyed the view for a while, then removed my clothing one item at a time on my way to the shower. No matter what I did, I had trouble regulating the pressure and temperature. Emerging with red skin on half of my body, I splashed cologne on my burns and facial stubble. I changed into an outfit designed for someone half my age, took a deep breath and looked in the mirror for a genuine excuse to stay home. I found none, and a few steps later the door closed behind me as I entered an evening of optimism and fear.

I passed through hordes of young men and equally rowdy women along the esplanade. I gave awkward smiles to fixed surveillance cameras and stood in a small cue. A bouncer looked me up and down, gave me a nod and I walked into the first club. Within two minutes I was back outside. The scene wasn't mine, but then again, what is?

The next secret door was called Old Berlin. This time, I stayed for almost half an hour talking to a couple of men celebrating their first year of marriage. They were expecting a child in six months from an overseas adoption agency. Such a far cry from the old system of life.

As I roamed aimlessly towards the beach-end of the mall, I witnessed a fight between three individuals. Two women scratched their male counterpart deeply before police broke them up. Soberly, I shifted my attention to the ocean waves breaking the shoreline in a fluorescent glow. Their energy took me away from the situation and seemed more organic than the faux paradise behind me. Absorbed in their perpetual motion, I was startled by someone tapping me on the shoulder.

'Julian.'

'Hey. Bliss.' I felt like I had sand on my tongue.

'Are you by yourself?' she asked knowingly.

'Yeah, I just wanted to get some fresh air and take a break from research. You know how it is.'

'It's always good to shake things up and get out of your head,' she said. 'Do you want to join us for a bit?' Her friends waited in the background like backup singers. 'Only if you want to, no big deal really. We're only going for a couple of drinks.'

'No, I don't think so, Bliss. I'll make my way back home soon.'

'Come on Julian, at least walk with us,' she urged. And like a tipsy school girl, she grabbed my arm and pulled me away from the lure of the ocean.

Her friends were pleasant enough. Young and easy on the eye. We strolled through the battlefield of loud youth and midlife revellers, stopping outside a pub-styled entrance that had steps leading below ground. I expected something more upbeat and funky.

'Come on,' Bliss said, 'just one drink with the girls.'

'I thought you didn't drink,' I questioned.

'Alcohol? No, I don't. But I like mocktails,' she clarified.

'I see.'

'Yeah, just a couple of drinks,' her friends sided.

Despite my initial hesitation, I accepted after further encouragement from the ladies. Once inside, the entourage mingled with other friends in the crowd. Bliss sipped on her fake stuff and I downed my first shot. Every so often one of the women unsuccessfully tried to drag me up to the dance floor.

'You don't dance, eh?' Bliss commented. 'There's no wrong move in dancing you know.'

'My mind and body are in tune with snow drifts and skiing, not computer generated beats,' I explained.

'That's a great perspective,' Bliss said. 'It must be very head clearing.'

'Have you not skied or experienced the Alps?'

'Skiing? Yeah, I guess I come from a privileged upbringing; I've been to a few snow resorts. But, I prefer to expose my skin to the elements, not cover it up.'

'We all have our differences,' I said. I had another shot and discovered the courage to ask Bliss what was always curious to me.

'Was it difficult to break away from your father's expectations of psychiatry and throw yourself into Cathedral with me?'

Bliss lifted her glass.

'Cheers to that!' she said and took a small sip before elaborating. 'It's been extremely confronting, that's for sure,' Bliss admitted. 'Looking back, I can see it might have been a rebellious thing. You see, despite being in love, my mother was constantly criticised by my father for being a hippie. For years Dad worked on her, until she become a "proper woman". It's sad, I can often sense her dissatisfaction of being a Stepford Wife, instead of the spiritual star child she identifies with. In fact, she named me "Bliss" in order to get some of her power back.'

'That's interesting,' I said. 'So your mother is Bliss and your father is Stone.'

'And I'm neither, because I am Bliss Celeste Stone.'

We corresponded a bit longer, and I allowed myself to be open to conversation. Something escaped my mouth, and she caught its dark humour. Bliss giggled, and I saw an aura around her head. It was the light of innocence; the spectre of higher intelligence and the energy of virgin virtues. A radiance that even the best photographers in the world will never be able to capture.

I got up and ordered another two drinks, leaving her behind with a playful frown on her much-too-young face. Upon my return she was being noticed by a good-looking man closer to her age. He made his move and began a conversation with her. I kept my distance and signalled that all was well. I offered my spare drink to a lady standing next to me.

'I'm with her,' I explained, pointing to Bliss with my head.

'Oh? Sorry about that.'

'It's all good. We're just friends and, just like this drink, she's too sweet for me. You look like you can handle it though.'

'Excuse me? Handle what?' She smiled playfully. 'The drink or you?'

The evening was turning out better than expected. Every woman in the room looked like sex and I was their god. I've never played this game of chance before. Beautiful strangers became long lost friends. This drug called fun appeared when my dignity dissolved. Even the victim inside me felt special.

A rock band thumped out post-punk remixes. All the girls who brought me here had left; except one. Constance clung to my arm as we swayed with the jolting crowd, just as the rock anthem dictated. I was skiing in an ocean of light and sound. In a place of comfort, Constance looked inviting. The blur of bright blue lipstick put my head in a spin, and I followed her bedroom eyes out into the open streets.

My ears were ringing, and I didn't hear most of what she said, but I nodded lots. She led me into a nearby apartment building and we rode the elevator to the ninth floor. I hate confined spaces, but I liked this one. Constance appeared to have a greater alcohol threshold than me, which I found curiously attractive. Filtering out the noise of too many drinks was near impossible as she pulled me towards a white, soft, leather lounge. For a few intense moments, my breath was caught between her tongue and my throat.

Constance then placed her hand on my knee to lift herself from the deep furniture. She headed towards the kitchen. I became confused and self conscious when she returned less playful. She steadily poured ice water into two glasses and handed me the fuller one.

'Do you pray, Julian?' she asked with a hint of cruel seduction. 'You know, like when you were a priest with a collar.'

I laughed. I really laughed out loud, which caught me by surprise. 'I never wore a collar. You watch too many movies,' I said. Constance gave me a fairy punch in the stomach and smirked. 'But no, actually, I don't pray the same way anymore.'

'Bliss mentioned you were a priest or something,' she revealed. 'Look at you now, Julian, all grown up.' She kissed me on the forehead and then sat on the floor opposite me. 'I'm still learning how to pray, but I find I get better results with open palms.'

Constance closed her eyes, took a deep breath and placed her hands face up on her thighs. I assumed she was showing me her flowery meditation technique.

'There, it's done,' she said. 'I just did it and nobody has to know about it.'

'Constance, you might have just created a recipe for one of the most challenging aspects of neurophysiology. Even my nerves feel better.'

'That's a big word, Julian. I'm not sure what neurophysiology means, but it's sexy as fuck.'

Constance uncoiled from her hippy pose and stood up.

'Feel free to air a bottle of red from the rack,' she said, 'I won't be long.'

It had been some time since I drank red wine; many years in fact. It was a personal protest because I associated it with drinking the blood of Christ. All the bottles looked the same to me so I chose one with a purple lid.

My hostess returned in a sexy, white nightshirt and a pair of pale blue, silk boxers. Her complexion appears more pale. She had removed some of her makeup and replaced it with a white foundation. Her blue lipstick was more electric now. A lamb in the company of a wolf. I remained composed and reminded myself that I'm the wolf and there is nothing fearful about lambs.

'Nice shorts.'

'They're very comfortable,' she replied. 'Are you?'

'Yes, very.'

I haven't experienced the company of a woman in this way for some time. I was unrehearsed. Suggestive music played in the background, the lights were dim, and I was pulled to my feet.

'Don't worry, Julian,' she said. 'Just stand still for a moment.' With uncertainty I took half a step back. 'Grrrr!' she growled and stepped forward. She stood on top of my feet and wrapped her long arms around my neck. Her curves swayed gently and her perfume overpowered the nightclub scent.

Fears of underperforming surfaced. I was not alone in my room anymore; this was real. My soul on the other hand was pushing for the experience. I relished each microsecond and tried to kill my insecurities.

The music and atmosphere turned more sexual, and the beat pulled us into each other. We began to grind. Swaying motions gave way to subtle thrusting actions. Our bodies rolled and connected with purpose. The softness of a woman produces a wealth of emotions, but I wanted to unleash a macho hardness, not a mummy's boy persona.

Poisonously sweet and hot breath permeated my stubble. Our mouths were open, but didn't connect. This was becoming an endurance sport.

Inevitably, our lips accidentally touched and it's a game changer. A gentle kiss. Constance was clearly the one directing me to the next level; however, she underestimated my appetite and I tested her commitment. Her body language told me to go further. My head and my crotch somehow united. I played the role of the alpha male; the first of my species to dominate Eve. My hand pushed the small curve of her lower back firmly towards me. My rules now; uncharted and unpredictable.

Holding my plaything with one hand, the other slowly explored a delicate body inquisitively. I had taken the form of an octopus; one that hides and sends out sensitive feelers. At my fingertips Constance fell into a state of hormonal limbo, as she marvelled in erotic torment at what might come next. I'm under pressure. I didn't want to disappoint her.

I calculated my next move like a psychopath.

Should I devour her now? No, play the game a bit longer, gain her trust, show some degree of affection.

I used one solitary finger against Constance's loose clothing to gently begin my domination. She responded with a slight quiver. My hand made its way south towards the valley of possibilities, but diverted northwards again just as things got too hot. I found a silky breast and skated around it before climbing an erect nipple, pressing against the thin fabric. She anticipated the next move and eagerly thrust forward. I took a small step back to let her know I'm taking full control. I sensed her torment and it heightened my arousal.

156

At long last I generously gave my prey a little something when I slid my hand inside her silken shorts and spread it over her cold cheeks. She reacted by forcing her vagina against my hard bulge, but still it wasn't enough for me to surrender all my sexual power.

Constance rested her head on my shoulder. In my mind's eye, she surrendered unreservedly to me. I placed one of my hands beneath her shirt and provided more assistance. She reached for my zipper.

'No,' I said firmly. She tried again. 'No!'

I thrusted my body towards her. Constance reacted with even greater arousal. Somehow she managed to take off her top and started to pull urgently on her shorts.

'Leave them on,' I said.

I directed her to a big glass window and stood behind her. We faced the city below. I dropped my jeans and closed the gap between us. Constance was forcefully nudged forward. I placed her hands slightly above her head and flattened her palms against the glass. I sensed her apprehension. I was inconsiderate about her exposure or other trivialities, such as window breaks. We were both highly charged in the moment, and I had no indication of a protest so I went for it.

The glass bowed slightly. Constance began to extend a hand towards me, as if to say 'pull back', but then changed her mind. Her hand promptly found its place again, and she pushed her backside against my erection. Within seconds, I slipped inside her through a leg opening of her loose boxers. A long-awaited deep moan fogged the glass. I eased in and thrusted deeper and slightly faster before easing off a bit. I took it in – this holiday from the usual self. It felt natural.

My mind is trained to analyse every situation and it began to override my pleasure again. I took swift action. I grabbed hold of Constance's shoulder and purposely-crafted hip and eased her against the windowpane. Her face and upper body were pressed flat against the transparent wall like a free advertisement in a seedy precinct. Between breathtaking views and shortness of breath, she made the unnerving choice to trust the stranger she invited into her home. The pendulum swings, for she was both regretful and grateful.

Constance made one last feeble attempt to push away from the window only to find my determined forward thrust colliding with her buttocks. She is thrown hard against the panel this time. Unharmed, she continued to play the game. Her sense of vulnerability seemed to excite her even more. One of her hands moved between her thighs, and I felt it enhance her pleasure. Her moans erupted in irregular shrieks as she neared her climactic end. She quivered repeatedly, and I felt her shudder for the last time before slipping my erect penis out of her body.

I stepped back and gently pulled her away from the window. I had a smug expression of gratification on my jowl. I'm wicked and felt like a man's man.

Constance dove onto the floor on a big, soft rug. I tugged my jeans up over my bulge and sat across from her with a glass of water in my hand. I gave her breathing space. She turned to my stupid, grinning face.

'What was that?' she asked in a tone I cannot fully define. 'Who the hell do you think you are, Julian, pulling a stunt like that?'

'The man you want me to be,' I replied arrogantly, as my analytical traits came back to torment me.

'Excuse me?'

'You like to be dominated by a strong authoritative personality, don't you?'

'What makes you think that?' she protested.

'Many things you told me throughout the evening,' I explained. 'I know you're self-assured, but you already told me you couldn't find comfort in younger men. Perhaps you are looking for a –'

'Huh? Nup! Stop! No way! I am not looking for a father figure and my childhood was just fine, thank you very much!'

There it is. The silence in the middle of a hurricane. The sound of my world crashing down all around me again. Constance looked to the floor and shook her head for reason, logic, and a way forward. I looked internally, and then heard laughter. Her refreshing, genuine easing of the situation.

'You idiot, Julian. It really has been a long time, hasn't it?'

She's okay, thankfully; however, I was descending into my world of detachment to all things emotional and personal.

Constance crawled towards me, and I felt so stupid. She kissed my forehead for the second time that evening. Self-consciously, I tried to cover up the shrivelling wet mess inside my pants as she extended one hand down to my lap.

Whatever punishment she dishes out, I deserve it. If she gets the biggest knife from the kitchen and places it against my throat, I'll hold my head still.

'Guess what, Mr Delusional, I'm not innocent or needy. You on the other hand have some serious issues to contend with.'

With my eyes closed, I felt the heat of her blue whispers against the side of my face, and her fingernails digging into my shoulder.

'You've obviously been deprived for some time,' she continued to taunt me, 'and I'm glad to help you out, Julian. God knows what you might have done to the next unsuspecting woman had I not accommodated your needs tonight and taught you right from wrong.'

It frightens the hell out of me to consider that she might be right. That my irrationality could have damaged someone. Another illusion of faith was destroyed and Constance was attempting to rebuild my confidence again by showing me forgiveness.

'Let me finish you off so you can leave your anguish behind when you leave here,' she says, like a true patron of the heart. 'You need this more than I do, but don't worry, Julian, I won't tell a soul you got it wrong, this time.'

Those words hurt. They cut deeply. I'm unclear who the victim really is here. I'm uncertain if any of this is healthy or not. Regardless, I needed to allow it.

I processed my conduct whilst Constance summoned the demon once more and retrieved my dignity with her skilled mouth. She captured my pain and generously swallows every last remaining trace of it.

I'm safe again, as long as I touch, but don't feel.

22

the nerve of humans

My office week began strangely, as if I were dancing blindfolded in a cemetery full of open graves. A juxtaposition of my life. I had no true indication whether Constance shared our experience with Bliss or not, but why worry about it? What did I gain from the glass-pushing exercise? I used a high building as a tool, as a decoy and prop, to distract her from my lack of sexual confidence. How self-centred have I become, and what lengths will I go to save face in the future?

My eye contact with Bliss Stone this morning was heavier than a Goth's eyeliner. I forced my head high enough to say something to her like an adult. I raised my voice loud enough to be heard, but my delivery was anything but perfect.

'You ready for our first patient?' I asked, in some lacklustre corridor of the Cathedral building.

'Julian!' She looked at me agape.

'What?'

'A greeting would be nice,' she responded.

'Oh, yeah, sorry. Everything good?'

'Yes. You?'

'Yeah, yeah, all good, yup!'

'You're not very convincing, but I guess that's your way sometimes,' she said. 'Now about our first patient, Jenna. Remember, she only responds to the name "Juniper", and her parents have some physical concerns that we need to address too. So please be a bit more sensitive than usual, Julian. Remember, she is young.'

'Yes, thanks for the overview, Bliss,' I responded, civilly. 'I can do sensitive.'

'Anyway, she has asked to be with you alone in the consulting room. She's given us no reason for this, but we need to respect her wishes. I won't be far if you need a female presence,' Bliss explained. 'I can watch on from the other room if you like.'

'Yes, I'd prefer you did,' I said. 'You never know with certain patients what their motives are.'

'Or yours for that matter,' she said. 'Good luck.'

Bliss and I are now equal business owners of our small clinic inside a section of Cathedral Haven, where she independently treats her own clients in a seperate office. Wherever possible, I still prefer her presence during my doctor-patient therapy time. This is not about her; it's for my ongoing co-dependency in the psychiatric environment. I don't trust myself with certain patients who suspiciously have similar traits to mine. There is sometimes a transference, common with many doctor/patient relationships, and it often takes on a sexual nature. Luckily, in all my years of practice, I have not needed to confront that obstacle with my clients.

I hit my session with a sense of dimensionality and personal struggle. This new patient had nerves attached to my own skin. Could someone please pass me a scalpel and nine banishing herbs? This was going to be tough!

'There is a misconception amongst you humans,' my patient remarked after our brief introduction.

'Are you not human yourself, Juniper?'

'I do not carry that weight of ignorance,' she said with disdain in her young voice. 'Julian, I must tell you that I can see straight through you.'

'Oh? And what do you see?'

'Vibrations and...'

'And...?' I waited.

'And I have overstepped my purpose here today,' she retracted. 'You will understand soon enough. Humans don't have a long physical life span; at least you're lucky in that respect considering the destructive nature of your kind.'

'When did this realisation that something is wrong with the world occur to you, Juniper?'

'The world is perfect, Julian, and there's certainly nothing wrong with perfection; for our Creator is altogether flawless. Humans like to think otherwise. They prefer to alter the state of perfection and upset the formula, because it's beyond them to consider themselves as something small and almost insignificant in the entire universe. They take the God concept and place it in their top pocket; our Creator is now the created. The Highest One is used as a bargaining tool, a measure for immorality, the ultimate weapon in the sick and feeble minds of the corrupted and insecure people that you on Earth call your leaders.

'I know your formula, Julian. You will ask me, "When did you recognise this, Juniper?". That is your next question. But it's all still part of the first question, so I'll continue to answer it for your benefit. I tell you something, Earth man, this blue marble has been watched for some time. We know your history better than your most senior historians, palaeontologists, scholars, and scientists combined. My kind, and many others too, have come to know earthlings as freaks that defy all sense of spiritual logic. Through a marriage of dust and vibration, the one you call God has given you paradise in an isolated corner of the universe so you can grow in a place surrounded by beauty and heavenly inspiration. You did not earn any of it. It was given to you through the thought of love. Now that you have it, not owing to any works, but from God's Grace alone, you destroy it by raping the land and waters and all the creatures within simply so you can exert your authority over all of God's living souls on Earth and beyond, including yourselves.

'What is even more remarkable is that the unique animals on Earth are widely revered by other intergalactic visitors. Many extraterrestrials come to your small globe just to observe the incredible wildlife, which is unlike any other because of the environmental balance needed to sustain such life. Obviously, it is difficult for us to hold back our disappointment when species after species is driven out of existence because of fake things you people call currency and ownership.

'How predictable that promises would be broken before satellites began to pollute the heavens when your leaders avowed "Space is for everyone – it has no ownership and is to be shared equally by all nations regardless of political preference". Now look at those contemptuous lies as technology progresses and greed is forever the motivator. Hostile nations remain pathetic in their own insecurities as they play stupid war games. Thousands of satellites litter outer space and the terrorism continues on the ground by "peaceful nations". Your expansion to dominate instead of accommodate is creating more vibrations for self destruction. You blast these "peace bombs" through the atmosphere using nuclear energy and the radiation fallout is eventually swept into the oceans and remaining forests, not to mention adrift in the universe.

'The people that ultimately suffer are those very ones that elected the psychopaths to power in the first place. Innocent creatures have no say in their slow, painful destruction.'

Juniper was fascinating to watch when she spoke. She had unnatural mannerisms. Her arms moved about in bursts of expression, rather than flowing movements. Her hands were almost claw-like and rotated at the wrist. I cannot recall a blink, not a natural looking one at least, just a double squint every now and then, as if she was learning to look natural. It was like she was being operated by an inexperienced puppeteer projecting a voice from another room.

'You're aware no full-scale war has broken out in some time, Juniper?' I asked.

'You are looking at this too literally, Earth man,' Juniper said. 'Outer space is littered with secret battles, especially in media domination and tracking services.'

I evaluated Juniper and her preachy patchwork, which is becoming a common trait amongst intellectual youth as they angst over generations of mistakes made by their forebearers. Some young adults take on the physical appearance of 'no gender aliens' by having their nipples and genitalia removed by surgery. The ultimate protest statement. Have there ever been contemporaries that haven't displayed anarchy in one form or another?

Admittedly, I rarely receive 'alien' youth; particularly one this physically, as in mannerisms, and emotionally absorbed in other lifeforms. I was talking to a young teen whose life had been interrupted by the insistent declaration that she is not an earthling. In my view, this alien adoption was not an issue of immediate concern, despite what her parents believed. However, there are other complications in response to this mindset that could lead to serious consequences in the future. Juniper's refusal to participate in earthly endeavours, including attending school and eating solid meals, was cause for concern if this phase continued much longer. Fortunately, at the moment, Juniper's problem-solving intellect seemed intact and her weight was in the healthy lower range for a fourteen year old of her height and body structure. According to her parents though, her weight was dropping dramatically.

'Do you understand the term "empathy" and its significance to the human condition?' I asked my patient.

'Yes, the ability to feel or identify with another living creature's pain,' she answered. 'It's a condition that many humans appear to be lacking in positions of power.'

'Why do you suppose that is, Juniper?' I questioned.

'Domination, pure and simple,' she replied.

Juniper was in good form, I was impressed. I also had something to work with. This teenager does not hold down a job and refuses to go to school, so I needed to ask myself where was this psychological profiling relevant in her life. I couldn't help but wonder if she was experiencing some very difficult times with someone at school, perhaps a senior teacher or somebody else in the educational system? Whoever it was, if it was, they would have to be at a level of high power for Juniper to have taken measures this far.

'Did you know it is now scientifically proven that psychopaths are lacking a part of the brain's chemistry, or at least have less of it than that of other individuals who show genuine empathy towards others?' I asked her.

'Yes, we have known about this deformity for some time due to our clinical observations during human sleep,' she said as a matter of fact. 'This masked condition should be tested amongst people before they have a career that is responsible for other people's general welfare in the workplace, and in society. All your science cannot detect the hidden agendas of these mutants. If someone suspects their boss to be psychotic there is very little to do except quit your job, your city, your state, your country, and hope the next place is free of the diseased mind.'

Juniper's mood had become increasingly emotional, as if she had personal experiences with these kinds of individuals. I knew I couldn't push too hard in that direction for now, therefore I decided to fish in another pond. I posed another question to her.

'Can your kind help humans?'

'The short answer is no,' she said. 'This is more a matter of cannot rather than won't, which is morally complex. Many galactic beings believe earthlings should be destroyed immediately, because it's obvious to us that you're all under some kind of polluted mindset. Your technology and weaponry is too advanced in the hands of fools. In fact, there are many other planets consisting of technologically less-advanced civilisations who are progressing more rapidly and spiritually than yours. You see, that is one of the biggest mistakes humans make – they are less spiritual as technology grows. It ought to be the other way around, because spirituality and the belief in the unknown opens doors to science. That is why your Earth scientists will never advance beyond that of other beings who integrate spiritual vibrations into their physics.'

'So, why don't you wipe us out?' I asked reasonably.

'Julian, you already know why, because then we would allow evil to do to us what it has already done to your planet. We are not going to compromise our Creator, we know our place in the whole scheme of things and that place is insignificant compared to the powerful force beyond your scope of vision. You have primitive powers, and your holy books teach your kind that the Earth is on pillars, a coffee table of all things. We know the Earth is simply vibration and we feel it wobbling out of control.'

'So ultimately you cannot help us because we need to help ourselves first in order to experience the shift towards growth and connection?' I summarised.

'To some degree,' Juniper confirmed. 'Although, I am having a conversation with you right now and giving you important information for your book, am I not? That is being helpful, is it not?'

'What makes you think I'm writing such a book?' I asked calmly.

'You're a student of psychiatry and philosophy – all doctors and professionals want to write books. It's human nature to share observations, but you must do something more.'

'What must I do, Juniper?'

'Tell it like it is and not what it appears to be like from a conditioned human's point of view. Don't be afraid to be absolute in your words because you never know when your soul will return to its home – be it a heavenly environment or a hellish one – and your successor will take up the project,' Juniper predicted.

I'm resilient, unwavering in my profession as a trauma observer. I had little reaction to the comments. My focus remained on the patient.

'Tell me about Heaven and Hell, Juniper.' I returned to her previous comment.

'The existence of both is very much a reality, although not in terms you earthlings understand it to be through your religious nonsense.'

'Oh? Well let's begin with Hell. Tell me, is Satan controlling Hell and torturing evil souls?'

'You silly Earth man,' she quipped. 'How could God's collective soul belong to Satan and why would our Creator give him such power?'

'Are you saying that Satan has no power in Hell?'

'Satan is simply a metaphor for a condition that seems to afflict you shady humans. It's a real entity, but not in the way that you are familiar with it. This evil condition is actually a lack of light – a lack of respect towards God's gift to you, and yourselves, which is most puzzling to us outsiders. Disrespect will catapult the worst of your kind into a state of Hell. Humans simply allow a metaphorical Satan to rob them of God's love. In turn, our Creator takes back what belongs to the light. God is in total control of both Hell and Heaven, as are you and all the other sentient beings.'

'That certainly makes more sense to me than the traditional theories,' I replied in a humanistic approach. 'But let's talk about you for a moment – where did your influences come from?'

'I told you, observing earthlings,' she said defensively. 'I'm not going to reveal anything about my ship or the vicinity of my planet or portal, but I will tell you that speed has very little to do with space travel.'

'Well, what does? Wormholes?'

'Yes,' she answered. 'You only need to get a piece of paper and mark two dots anywhere on it to see how Einstein's loophole works. Two worlds can easily become connected instantly no matter how distant they are in a straight line.'

'You know Einstein was an earthling?' I responded.

'So was Tesla, but neither of them were your traditional scientists and both of them were open to suggestion,' she said. 'Tesla was persecuted for his genius, and perhaps we showed him too much too soon. As far as wormholes go, it's a blessing to us visitors that you still observe things from a three-dimensional model.'

'Interesting concept,' I granted, 'but now consider my observation for a moment. You resemble a teenager, Juniper. Does that signify that you took on this form on purpose?'

'Of course Julian!'

'So if I stabbed you with a sharp implement you would bleed?'

'Yes, and I will no doubt experience pain too. There is no point in studying the workings of a mind if you are only at arm's reach of the subject. I suspect you have firsthand experience with what I'm talking about and that's all the more reason to be honest with your findings.'

'Granted, that is sound reasoning; however, surely you must know where we humans have gone wrong if you have entered someone's soul?'

'No, no, no, Julian, we cannot enter and overtake anybody's soul, nor would we want to do so,' she protested. 'That's God's domain and that of the individual who leases that space. We don't want to catch the same disease as you humans. Can you imagine the destruction we could cause if we abandoned our essence to coexist with earthlings? It's not an attractive proposition.'

I sat up and took control of my domain. I glanced down at a piece of paper where I had written a name before I entered this conversation with a brilliant child claiming to be an extraterrestrial. The name on Juniper's birth certificate and medical files clearly stated that she was in fact fourteen-year-old Jenna Anne Pierce. I don't think Jenna is in danger of self harm. She is in no danger to herself or that of others. There are many vegetarians in the world, and Jenna seems to be maintaining her nutritional intake for now. In many ways the teenager has shown great fortitude and if not for the alien fantasy, which I believe she will grow out of depending on her parents' behaviour, her future looks positive in a leadership role.

'You have so much passion about your observations, Juniper,' I said, 'and I thank you for sharing it with me today. Your friends in your physical age-group are not generally able to stay focussed on deep philosophies for extended periods, as you are fully aware, and this is through no fault of your own. You are simply ahead of your time. I suggest dropping a couple of IQs when in their company and you will experience more comfort in this form you have taken on here on Earth. But never, like all the geniuses in this world and the next, get comfortable with mediocre. Look beyond just experiencing this moment, see your human grow in the future too.'

For the first time during the session, Jenna absorbed some of my observations. I saw the portions of opportunity getting larger, therefore I cut the slices thicker than before and handed her some food for the soul.

'I know the rubbish they teach you in strict schools. I know the feeling of suffocation when you hold your sacred truth in a locked room full of unsettled dust and fractured peers. I know the physical and psychological strain that a psychopath in a place of authority can put you through. I can really identify with you about the way an outsider would view the human race with all of its scars. I can empathise with you when you want nothing to do with any of it.

'You are certainly an incredible creature with some cutting edge observations, and it makes no difference to me if you are an alien or a schoolgirl. Your words are enough to lift my curiosity and evaluate the real struggles we as humans have in this chronically suppressed landscape of ours. You, being an alien and all, would be aware that if one goes around declaring that they are from another planet then further persecution will only arise and all your valid points will go unheeded by a closed society. Therefore, it would be in your best interest, and that of our future society, to pretend that you are who your parents think you are and evolve slowly into a leader with a clear message when the human form you are in matures enough to be independent of your host family. Do you see my angle, Juniper?'

I was unsure how this talk was going to affect my patient or my reputation, but I had to trust my life experiences. Being human has taught me how to deal with humans and extraterrestrials alike, without fear of losing consciousness.

'Yes, I see your approach clearly, Julian. Well played,' she said. 'Are you going to tell my adopted parents that I'm crazy and need further assessment?'

'No,' I replied. 'I will recommend that as long as your physical health is not at risk then there is no need for alarm. I'm also going to recommend that your parents listen to what you have to say because I certainly find your comments of the utmost interest and it could lead to a prosperous future. There are special colleges that cater for students of advanced initiatives and that encourage free thinking. I'd certainly offer you a reference if you wish to consider this option after some discussion with your parents.'

'Thank you, Julian. That sounds reasonable,' she said.

'My pleasure, Juniper.'

'I have learnt something from you today.'

'And what is that, Juniper?'

'You cannot remember me because you are too busy trying to fix people too.'

23

charity case

I cannot determine if it was Juniper who planted the idea of alienation in my mind or if it came voluntarily. My lack of organic connection to society has raised some needs lately, and I feel compelled to step up and reconnect with the people on the outer edges of acceptance; the ones who have no fixed address or a reason to trust.

I recently attended a homeless appeal that was so successful in its first year that it earned a staggering amount of money for its charity. This was a far cry from decades earlier where support for the destitute and poverty stricken were somewhat of a burden for corporates, rather than an opportunity to leverage business profits and help those in need at the same time.

Business minds pooled together to raise money for the needy by offering a sleep out to CEOs in an undercover sports stadium. I thought this fundraiser would be a sleeping bag on the ground with very little luxuries. However, the event, which took place a few days before the end of the financial year, was an unrealistic farce in many respects. Apart from my unlimited hot beverages and cups of soup, there was also food available for a donation. The choir and entertainment kept me up longer than I wanted, but at least I had access to very clean restroom facilities and a roof over my head on my padded floor, unlike true struggling homeless people. I still use some of the sponsored items in my show bag, as part of my participation on the night. Yes, CEOs deserve a bit of praise for raising money and awareness, but my invitation to an exclusive cocktail party at a high class venue a week later was thrown in the WTF? trash. That money could have been used better to shelter more people, not to funnel it back to the ones who donated in the first place.

I try to keep on top of the growing number of volunteer organisations in my local area. This knowledge is vital, because many patients are afflicted with issues better treated through continual support by an active co-op rather than a one-on-one consultation with me. Friendship and acceptance goes a long way in the healing process.

Bliss Stone has also participated in a charitable experience that Keith Rhode directed us to. Petal routinely drives their fleet of stocked vehicles to various locations and hands out food parcels to the needy. However, Bliss found out that Petal is more than a mobile soup kitchen for vagrants.

Homelessness by definition is quite ambiguous. Bliss learnt that a home is a place of protection and privacy; a complete sense of belonging. In contrast, a shelter is nothing more than a roof over one's head; there is no special sense of belonging. Conclusively, prisoners, street people, and even homeowners themselves can fall into the condition often referred to as 'homelessness'.

Although the course that Bliss attended strongly emphasised Christian morals and principles, even utilising Scripture and prayer during the program with a feel of a sermon at times, the charity clearly does not discriminate between different faiths. In fact, the religious consortium stipulates to their volunteers never to preach or try to convert patrons. This is mainly due to previous misgivings and because this approach could become counterproductive if attempted by inexperienced members. If the client is searching for Scriptural wisdom then he or she can be directed to an experienced member of the faith for guidance.

Safety is a top priority in such organisations and so too are legal issues. Under common law, a priest or their equals in such roles are not required to inform police of any confessions of a criminal nature, no matter how serious that crime might be. A volunteer with no religious title on the other hand could be charged with being an accomplice after the fact if he or she does not surrender information upon request by law enforcers. These regulations have compromised many staff members and patrons alike.

Bliss Stone was told that any information she is privy to must not be released to the public without permission from the charity because Petal holds close to secrecy. This might sound odd, but charities are in a competitive marketplace and funding is always being cut by governments. The law is the law and we must remain prudent with all of her findings. All circumstances, names, locations, and discussions will be altered here before any of it goes public in a journal, which I'll compile later, to avoid legal repercussions. For this purpose though, I will keep it real for you because you hitched a ride with me on this journey of truth and discovery.

Besides absorbing all this new information on the ins and outs of running an outreach business, Bliss also took note of the scores of volunteers who attended the program. People from a cross-section of our society chose to give a few hours of their life per week to the homeless cause. Despite this noble intent, Bliss could not help but make professional observations during her interactions and psychological profiling. She felt that other powerful motivational factors may have given the recruits the incentive to help others who were 'needy'.

'Some of these people are going through the motions for self reasons rather than that of the collective,' she noted. 'After all, where would the motivation be if we did not feel the drive from within our own anguish?'

This concept of helping others so we can help ourselves is not a new one. During a broadcast of a recent tsunami recovery program oversees, Ravine Arcane made mention in her notes of an Australian medic. The surgeon commented on national television that she loved going to such devastated places because she lived for it and it made her 'feel powerful and special'. These strong motivational reasons go relatively unnoticed by the general public, yet when a national radio station was criticised for making similar observations on airtime they were crucified for it.

Since when is it a crime to feel psychosocially empty unless you help victims? I know what that condition feels like. If you recall, I'm here to help you because I'm the one who desires the feeling of belonging. I too am homeless despite having shelter, food, and other physical comforts. The way of the word is upsetting, as Juniper highlighted previously, and that's an unhealthy mindset unless we carry that burden with some proaction.

Bliss's initial charity information night was Petal's largest turnout for some time in the local area. About fifty volunteers signed up and paid their registration on the first evening. No surprise considering the plight of the homeless has been featured heavily in social media of late. Bliss settled in, observed, and interacted. Christmas was approaching, and she noted that some people get involved with charitable work during Christmas time in order to fill a temporary void in their life, which might extend into the New Year.

'We always get a few individuals that fall off the radar,' the director reminded the eager group, 'but that's human nature. For many who take up this challenge, it would seem like a good idea at the time.'

Bliss liked his honesty and was aware she too was going to fall off the radar. Firstly though, she needed to gain enough information to help us develop a better understanding of what's out there for our clients, and for us in our continual development of strategies. She informally highlighted some of her findings and I hijacked her statements.

The New Year arrived and the dropouts went back to their familiar lives. The term 'commitment' has lost its momentum for most of the volunteers now and 'Christian values' and 'Christmas appeals' no longer serve them as reason for continuing with this kind of humanitarian work. All's not lost however, as a few extraordinary individuals continue to be rewarded in their chosen cause and an appreciation for a delicate balance in their lives prevails.

Of those who abandoned their initial calling, the cycle of searching for fulfilment continues in other areas. I know this to be true because I have had contact with a few of these individuals via social media. Some have found another cause – another purpose.

Whether one belongs to an organised charity or not, it does not govern their real worth. Choices are simply another form of personal attitudes. This should never be driven by guilt or hype. These are still early days into my research and I'm about to taste my first real charity role in a different environment away from the street food vans and soup kitchens.

Initially during her course, Bliss prematurely assumed that her service would only be delegated to one of the mobile kitchens stationed at parks during evening hours. As it turned out, there were many more options available to volunteers and she decided to go into an area she knew nothing about.

The courthouse was the last place she expected to rally for charity. Bliss experienced the following situations whilst it was freshly brewing in the melting pot that is our legal system, but has since been removed from service altogether.

It began with the first official outreach roster after Bliss had already dedicated some of her evenings with mobile food vans. She ticked a box to volunteer for a morning schedule at court where drug offenders were to appear before magistrates. She had no idea of what to expect. Her imagination painted images of skinny, pasty-faced drug addicts and organised crime figures, but that was inexperience talking.

Two veteran volunteers had been assigned to the courthouse along with three others from the recent recruiting drive. Bliss was the only new recruit to show up. The role consisted of offering hot drinks and light snacks to nervous people awaiting their time before a judge. Bliss noted right away of how a little gesture like this helped decrease anxiety in those awaiting appearance. Trish, the team leader, explained how some people will open up whilst others sip on their drinks without uttering a word.

The 'drug court' title is misleading because it's more accurately a 'drug reform' program with policing policies in place rather than a conventional court appearance. This trial procedure is designed to help repeated drug-related criminals stay out of jail, and it's not a service offered to all offenders because of funding shortfalls. Despite an offer of clemency through the drug court system, many prisoners prefer to stay in jail rather than have conditional freedom handed to them. It seems, some addicts have a dependence to drugs that far outweighs the program's requirements.

After a busy couple of hours, the three Petal staff sat in their little room and made small talk whilst relying on a directional signpost to show patrons the way to free refreshments. A known middle-aged man walked in and asked for a coffee. One of the ladies commented on his calf muscle tattoo. She said, in an unflattering way, that it looks like he self-etched it onto his skin himself. Bliss braced herself for some kind of reaction.

'Oh that?' he responded. 'Yeah, I was really bored that day and I did it in class when I was in high school. Got expelled for it.

'I can tell you did it yourself because of its position – like you sat down and rested your leg against the other at a right angle.'

'Yeah, that thing is as old as me,' he joked.

'Your birthmark,' Bliss commented with a smile, which was reciprocated.

'You should see my back,' he said. 'They're much better.' He lifted his shirt to display more raw artwork.

'Where did you get those done?' Trish asked.

'Half in prison and the rest at home,' he replied.

It was at that point that Bliss reminded herself that she had been talking to people either doing time or on some kind of release condition. Some of which were hardened criminals. This man did not fit the stereotype mould and a pattern was forming. There is no visible mark that separates a convicted prisoner from a free person.

A skinny youth swimming in a shiny, black tracksuit and body sweat walked into the room looking somewhat on edge. He asked for a hot chocolate.

'How many spoons of chocolate powder?' Roslyn asked.

'Eight,' he said softly and helped himself to some biscuits.

'Eight? What about sugar?'

'Nah.'

He departed immediately with no intention of further communication.

Moments later a young man entered the open room. He was known to both Trish and Roslyn, but they waited for him to initiate any formal conversation. The man was neat in appearance and seemed 'clean' and intelligent. He sat down in a chair next to Bliss whilst another slightly older man, dressed professionally, stood at the doorway with a branded takeaway coffee cup. Bliss assumed the man in the suit was a lawyer. The seated male asked for a Milo/coffee mix and stretched out his arm to grab a piece of carrot cake.

The conversation began to trickle, and he asked if the three women were all volunteers. Roslyn made it clear that none of them were paid for their services. Bliss mentioned that it was her first time in this capacity and was still confused about the whole concept of the reform program. Openly, the young man explained his circumstances and how this opportunity was transforming his life within the system.

The semi ex-con was familiar with the role of the charity that Petal serves in the community, as he had seen the fleet of mobile kitchens at numerous locations, including the jail in which he served time. This stranger never revealed his name, but he did leave his story for Bliss to absorb.

The odds of criminal activity were stacked up against him from an impressionable age. Both of his parents were heavy drug addicts. His habits of petty crime were followed by heavier criminal activity. Stints in juvenile homes progressed, and he had lived behind bars for most of his adult life.

'I don't understand?' Bliss said. 'Lots of people take drugs and don't spend that much time behind bars.'

The fellow took pity on her slow logic and earnestly explained that he resorted to armed robberies to support his addiction, much like many desperate drug addicts do eventually. The picture didn't seem to fit somehow. This guy seemed extremely pleasant and physically attractive. He did not look like a man who would hold a gun to someone's head. But that was the whole point. Without the addiction, this man might not have gone to those desperate measures.

The criminal stopped to reflect for a moment whilst Bliss still processed the imagery of a hold up in her mind.

'I never thought I was doing any harm to anyone except myself until I was offered this new program,' he said.

Bliss informed me that he impressed the three women with his openness, mannerisms and charm. Unfortunately, they were in no position to judge, only to serve.

'Do you come here weekly?' Bliss asked, unsure exactly, but probing too much in her volunteer position.

'When I first started I did. Now I come fortnightly. This is the longest I've been free from drugs,' he explained.

'How long?' she asked.

'Four and a half months,' he revealed proudly.

Bliss congratulated him and asked more questions about his experiences in the program, beyond her supporting role as coffee and cake provider.

'I see Judge Downing,' he explained in part. 'I have lots of respect for that man and I think that's the reason I'm getting on top of my addictions. I feel supported.' He threw his empty, throwaway cup into the wastepaper basket. 'I have a diary I fill out and they do a medical test here every time I appear. I think they have a lab here somewhere. My results come back right away.'

'Do you find the diary helpful?' Bliss continued to probe.

'Writing things down definitely helps me enormously.'

'So, they – the decision makers – read your diary?' she asked.

'No, no one does,' he informed her. 'I just tell them of any concerns or problems and we work together in finding a solution, or back in I go! I'm responsible for all my actions and this is probably my last chance to break the drug cycle I have.' The man in the suit re-entered through the doorway.

'It's time to go,' the man said.

'Okay. Thanks for the drink, ladies,' he said and disappeared in the system again.

'Sometimes they open up and sometimes they don't,' Trish repeated her earlier comment. 'There's another fellow I've spoken to on occasion and has probably finished the trial by now. He had nothing but praise for this initiative too. Although, he did say not everyone benefits. Even if a small number get through it's still worth the effort and money, I think.'

'Lots of these people are so genuine, like that fellow that just left, and it's plain to see the positives,' Roslyn added with a voice of experience.

A slim young lady poked her head in the doorway and asked if there was a café in the building. Her eyes darted across the room to avoid face contact.

'No, not in this building,' Trish said, 'but we've got free tea and coffee. What would you like, dear?'

'Help yourself to some cake too.' Bliss raised some slices and placed them in front of her.

'A coffee would be nice. White and three, thanks.' She gained the confidence to look at Trish and said that her friends were probably interested in a coffee too and she would let them know of the service.

Before the lady left the room with her coffee, Bliss urged her to take some biscuits down to her friends, after she observed her eyeing them off.

Petal is also involved with correctional facilities and gives inmates opportunities to approach the van on prison grounds. This kind of association is perhaps the most delicate, in that hardened inmates take caution to associate with outsiders. Usually because of retribution from other inmates. Nevertheless, for those women and men from various detention centres who make the decision to connect, it gives them a lift. It takes a courageous Petal staffer to be able to reach out to someone in these concrete and metal environments. Petal is often the only link to the outside world for many of these inmates and the only light they might be experiencing in the grey world of prison life.

Bliss Stone returned to Cathedral Haven and resumed her normal duties after another morning in court. This was her last callout for Petal, as she has gathered enough information and has now disappeared off their radar like so many others before her. One of the latest developments, which nobody seems to talk about much at the charity, is the effects of gambling on people's lives.

Increasingly, we have become numb to the pokies equation in mental health. People from all walks of life have turned to crime in order to support their poker machine addictions. This pokies drug is responsible for many marriage breakdowns, financial ruin, serious crimes, health issues, nutritional neglect, homelessness, and parental neglect, amongst other destabilization. The lawmakers have not prohibited this extremely addictive drug, but in fact encourages this form of 'entertainment' because of revenue collection. We have seen this disease eat into the lives of some of our own customers. Not to be lured into a pokies den, and stay clean when there's a legal dealer at every corner, is almost impossible for the vulnerable.

Bliss had seen many variations of poverty in her short time with Petal. Without much effort, she spoke to a mother in her twenties during one of her earlier food van outings. The woman had two toddlers living with her in a rusted sedan in a public car lot. Physically surviving only thanks to charitable organisations, but dying psychologically due to public condemnation. It was against the rules, but Bliss offered her free counselling sessions to try and get her mind clearer for the future. It was particularly disturbing to see that her car was parked across an embankment of a well-known brothel.

24

vital signs

On one of my bicycle rides I followed the sound of music to an area on the foreshore of my neighbourhood. There was a concert in town. It was no Woodstock, and the gathering was very sparse. I pulled up on a patch of grass and sat down. Within seconds I was approached by people who began asking questions and laying down scriptures. Some even wanted to pray for me. They moved on as quickly as they arrived after I told them I was studying the effects of harassment in public spaces.

I recognised one of my former patients, Pam, in the wings when one of the songs was winding up with the 100th hallelujah hitting a high note. She had come to us seeking ways to block out her horrid past. I informed her that the past would forever be a part of her experiences and trying to block it out would only lead to other psychological problems. All she needed to do was recognise that even in the most darkest hours, she remained perfect. I enforced that she didn't need to prove anything to anyone. I hadn't seen Pam in some time, so I was curious to know how she had been getting on since she stopped her appointments at the clinic.

I looked around the grounds and saw Bibles and hands reaching for the clear sky. The relatively small crowd was catching the spirit of Jesus through their fingertips and needy souls. I anticipated emotional frenzies would follow.

Pam noticed me on the grass and made her way to my solo camp. She arrived with a hairless fellow dressed in a black T-shirt, black trousers, and black joggers. Pam introduced him, rather proudly, as Michael, then informed me he was totally deaf.

'Michael does incredible work for the Lord despite his physical disability,' she informed me.

I sensed that Michael had no interest in me or my profession. After some smalltalk, smiles, and head nods, Pam walked away proudly with her fashion accessory by her side. I watched her move towards the stage in her designer heels and white cotton pants. Her loose fitting orange blouse massaged my eyes with its silkiness and softened the harsh opinions I had created of their partnership.

A woman approached the podium. The anticipation of another inspirational speech about being saved sent the increasing gathering into a series of excitable whispers. I couldn't help but gaze at this strikingly beautiful woman. If I had the ability to look into a person's soul, I would have used it then, because this was a curiosity. The lady on stage had an innocence and demure persona that radiated genuine peace and goodwill to all, and yet she had not spoken a word. On the other hand, as a man, I might have been attracted to the women who I sensed needed 'fixing'. It was a dreadful thing to consider, but unfortunately many damaged men feel this way about women and they are forever looking for damaged goods to repair so they feel better about their own blemishes.

For the first time, I had blocked out the noise of the crowd and the distracting energy they produced. The lady stepped closer to the microphone, but she was not alone. An older female was clinging to her hand and offered emotional support. There was a long awkward delay. The aide stepped up and briefly introduced Evelyn and broke the silence. They hugged and she stepped back again, leaving the guest speaker to talk to the patrons. It was enough, and Evelyn began to talk with a shaky, but captivating naturalness. She immediately struck harmony with the individuals at the Jesus rally, and even I became totally absorbed. I didn't feel the sun burning into my skull or notice the huge yachts stealthily sailing past in the seaway anymore. Not even the gorgeous, clear blue sky that painted three hot air balloons on its canvas could distract me from such mysterious beauty.

Evelyn pulled away from the microphone slightly after her initial greeting and short introduction. Her support lady was audibly heard saying, 'It's okay, you're doing great,' and further encouraged her to share her story of inspiration to the believers, and me.

When Evelyn returned to the microphone she uncovered layers of her life that were extremely heavy and toxic. I listened like a psychiatrist would, but also became affected like any individual with empathy would. This experience was good for me, because it did not take place in a clinical office and I was under no obligation to find solutions to her deeply psychological issues. I was simply a listener caught up in a stranger's story.

Evelyn detailed the outer city meth labs of her old home state. She was constantly neglected and abused in volatile living conditions. Shortly before she hit her first teenage years, she was a runaway. But nobody was searching. She figured it was safer on the streets than living with unpredictable parents and the company they kept.

The Cross, a known district for sex workers, eventually seemed like a natural progression soon after. It didn't take long for a scout to notice the desperate, innocent child and introduce her to a friend, a drug, then a way to temporarily sustain that drug habit. Her body was always for hire but her mind closed rapidly, as one immoral situation rolled into the next.

As a matter of survival, Evelyn believed she had no choice other than to rob herself of a childhood and allow dirty fuckers to pollute her chemically distorted undeveloped body. Her sense of self and any spiritual connection to the world was buried beneath a layer of rapidly aging skin and panda eyes.

Now in her early thirties with perfect deportment skills, Evelyn stood tall in front of the spellbound audience explaining how she once allowed herself to be degraded by numerous strangers of all different backgrounds. She would have done anything to stick a dirty needle in her arm; her legs were accustomed to open at the drop of a note, and her knees would bend at the rattle of loose change.

Her talk was more suited to a private venue, I thought, and I doubted these folks were prepared for something this real and confronting. It was refreshing, despite its pain, that somebody could actually reveal sincerity rather than censorship.

In moments of murky clarity, Evelyn found her own actions to be degrading and disturbing during her desperate binges. Despite all these upheavals, the child kept playing seedy adult games, and by the time she reached legal digits the junkie prostitute wore signs of escape on her wrists, just below the bruised pits in her arms.

After a string of abusive attacks, Evelyn attempted to go cold turkey and in a vague, dry stupor escaped the shackles of The Cross and a relentless pimp. She landed hard on soft sand in another State, not far from where I found G long ago. But it didn't end there. Addiction does not recognise geography. New vultures moved in and mounted her like a lifeless carcass; just another piece of meat to clients and an open artery for opportunistic dealers.

Evelyn spoke from experience and articulated her autobiography in a juxtaposing landscape. I saw her dignity intact and wasn't processing what the others thought of her performance.

Evelyn revealed the mindset of an abandoned, beautiful person who lived in the depths of a manufactured hell. And, why such a person was reluctant to leave that place of torment. The forces that kept the body from escaping this nightmarish existence were complex. Interestingly, the term 'Satan' or 'devil' had not surfaced in her sermon, perhaps because Evelyn accepted responsibility for her own actions and choices. A highly religious person would perhaps never understand such striking truths of self judgement and personal growth, but why was she here at the event if not to be part of the Christian crusade?

Evelyn then spoke of a 'knight in shining armour', a bald man dressed in black. Evelyn spoke passionately of how Michael and a few other volunteers searched the sand dunes along the beaches for troubled souls to save. They came across her in a deplorable state. She turned to the man in black, who stood right of stage, and spoke.

'This angel, with his kind face and gentle nature, introduced me to Jesus!'

At that she swept her arms around the gentleman and allowed emotion to finally catch up to her. The crowd applauded and euphoria followed with echoes of 'Amen!' The gathering had increased threefold.

Something within me snapped back into place. My sense of critical reasoning suddenly hit other notes. The sounds of the crowd drowned a real story. I know the power of injecting scripture, and I have seen the devastation that street drugs cause. In my mind, both are addictive and both have the capacity to be soul destroying. Finding Jesus often fills the heart with illusions. Jesus did not save these people – people save people, point blank!

The goodwill of individuals is often overlooked and the push to thank institutions and invisible idols is forever present. I was both saddened and happy for Evelyn. I just hoped she could one day truly find herself without the crutch of others and their special needs.

I tried to hold my thoughts from spinning out of control. Was I jealous that I hadn't found her first? That I could have shown her an alternative to the men in black? My split reasoning continued, and I questioned the soundness of why a person like Evelyn felt the need to confess her past transgressions to a group of strangers who would reasonably never be in such a situation. I could only speculate that the lady craved acceptance by those that she considered to be the pillars of our society; a morally ethical community known as Christians. These Jesus re-birthers would find it difficult to have found a better ambassador than Evelyn to speak their truth. They had struck gold and wore it proudly.

The flock walked away from that gathering feeling touched by the divine experience. I felt something too – an emptiness.

The impact these knights in black had on such desperate people set my soul alight. It sounds harsh, I know, but I was one of them once. I wasn't the solution. The faith I pushed onto desperate people was no substitute for personal and honest responsibility. The power we all have as individuals is far greater than the largest congregation ever assembled. I came into this world alone, without human flesh, as did you, and I will exit alone without my flesh, as will you without your baggage. Therefore if anyone tells you that they know of secret things, then they are an imposter because they do not even know themselves. If Jesus is our measuring stick, then questions remain: Who is doing the measuring, and what is the real motivation behind such calculating measures.

25

predator

Regression therapy reveals overwhelming responses in some patients who will have a harder time handling the information. Quite often I choose to simply have a conversation with my client depending on my mood, the kind of energy I feel that person has, and the age of the sufferer. Despite what you might think, ethics is actually important to me.

Although Bliss is now an independent master in her field of psychoanalysis, she still respects that I would like her present in some of my sessions from time to time. Perhaps she is keen to observe because she now has skin in our little practice, and wants to make sure I don't go too radical with my treatments. This remains true when young people seek psychological assistance, especially when something sits between brain science and fantasy.

The eleven-year-old boy we were about to meet is very special because there is nothing outwardly special about him. I don't have too much information about him on record, but what I do have is a sense of knowing. I have some kind of connection to the things he feels.

Bliss only knows what is written in the report. The boy, known as Stem, has visual disturbances that are beginning to affect him socially, which makes it increasingly difficult to prolong friendships and 'fit in'. Stem is becoming distant to the environment around him, and some other obsession is overtaking his life.

Stem's father waited outside whilst Bliss and I eased into the session with his son. But the session, from a clinical point of view, was nothing more than a chat. There was no reason I could see to delve deep into Stem's claims because in a sense I know what kind of things he is going through based on my own adolescent dealings. As a child, all I wanted was someone to listen and acknowledge that my experiences were real, not to be shut down with medical reasons of why it's all in my head. The most important thing Stem needed was to simply tell his story, or at least a part of it, without judgement or opinions. If he was old enough, I would have offered him a scotch and listened to him unravel until he was free of knots.

Bliss and I were very encouraging, and Stem was remarkably confident and articulate, giving lots of detailed information when he spoke. His story moved in the following way.

Stem's biological clock woke him well before other kids in his neighbourhood. His family home is nestled between the outer suburbs of the city and the track to nowhere. His mother and father had already left for work and it takes them over an hour to get to their different jobs. His mother works as a cleaner in a hotel and his father is barely holding on to his sheetmetal position at a small factory.

Stem turned on his light and pulled open the curtain. The mirrored image of himself on the window gave him a small fright. Water trickled down the inside of the glass like tears of sadness. He placed his finger on it and drew a smiley face. He was pleased that darkness and heavy fog absorbed the landscape outside. Stem knew he had a much better chance of being the first kid at school in these ominous conditions.

After downing his sugary breakfast cereal, Stem took another look outside, from the lounge room window this time. A white-grey haze was suffocating the fence line, which signalled that it was time to move and claim his title as early bird champion. He threw his backpack on his shoulder and stepped out into the thick, cold, low cloud. Everything was still and quiet. It felt particularly eerie once he got to his letterbox. He couldn't see the end of the street, which was a mere three houses away. Stem turned towards his house and briefly reconsidered his decision. The brown corner brickwork of his bedroom wall drifted away from him, sinking into a deep, milky ocean.

Stem had been going through some problems at home. His brother was giving him a hard time, typical of pre-teen siblings, but it was more than that. Without adult care, Stem felt unsupported. His parents were locked in a huge mortgage, he told us in his own way, and they kept telling him they needed to go to work to pay the bills. He understood that but it still hurt.

Stem pushed forward into the white abyss and kept calm by focussing on the outcome rather than the cause. He turned a corner not far from home when he felt a strong presence following him. Despite his best efforts he could not see a soul through the thick blanket of fog. There were no dogs barking; no cars running; no sounds of children or adults getting the day underway. Many of the houses were still under construction and unoccupied. One building after the other appeared in surreal watercolour shadows as Stem moved from one driveway to the next. He had never seen his new suburb in this light before. Something was definitely changing. The excitement of a new housing estate suddenly felt morose.

A noise entered the silence; the distinct sound of flapping wings travelled close by and then stopped somewhere above the road. Stem looked up to see a silhouette of an oversized bird standing on one of the lamp posts, which was not in use. He estimated its size to be 'prehistoric' and large enough to cause him some serious harm. He closed his eyes and took a few steps whilst counting to ten in his head, hoping it would disappear. After he opened his eyes again, he stopped in complete silence and looked around. The thing had moved on. That wasn't the end of it though. Several minutes into his walk the bird-like creature returned about one block away from the school gate. Stem took in a deep breath and coughed up cold biting air. This bird thing spread its wings and glided into the direction of the playground. Stem, with some reluctance, followed.

He walked into the empty grounds, which were layered in heavier fog and shadowy shapes. It seemed much colder too. It wasn't the buzz Stem was hoping for. A rising fear he had never experienced crawled inside him when he realised that he had to stay put for some time before anyone showed up. He considered hiding in places, such as between buildings, but that would mean venturing further into the belly of this alien city. He created an image in his mind and saw a faceless person waiting for him there, someone who wished to cause him unimaginable harm.

Stem decided to wait it out under the assembly hall because he could have a better view of the grounds and main gate if this fog lifted, should anyone approach. He nervously waited and anticipated the second kid stepping up onto the lonely podium, but something else stood before him instead.

It was huge, that bird-like creature, and it stood fearlessly in the middle of the assembly area, like a mythical guardian. It looked straight at the lone child. It had glowing red eyes that pierced through the haze. This animal of another civilisation, another time, seemed to have an intelligence other beasts didn't. It had abilities of telepathy, and Stem was trying to work out the message it was sending whilst trying to block it out at the same time. He tried not to look at the humanoid crow-like stalker, but he could not deny its energy.

The gravity of the situation made his stomach churn, like a composting pile of undigested waste was eating away at him. Stem held back the sick and drifted elsewhere as if having a near death experience, where time stood still long enough to process the situation in one slice of thought. He had to weigh up what was more important: status or safety? A very real predator could be lurking in this surreal landscape. This game of hide and seek had become extremely disturbing and 'stranger danger' were the words that came to mind.

An unusual piercing sound sent Stem back into the head and heart of the situation. In front of him stood the biggest crow he had ever seen. Another familiar form took shape, the shape of an angel, and the bird took flight with its expansive, black wings leading the way for the child to follow.

Stem ditched his bag and ran out of the school gates. The shadowy stalker was invisible to Stem on his way home, but he was certain the dark guardian was closely keeping watch.

Later that morning, Stem did what most kids do, such as watch the morning cartoons and throw a tennis ball against the wall of his brother's bedroom. Zappa eventually emerged and pegged the ball at Stem's face before firing up the stove for his traditional eggs and bacon breakfast. Zappa had his routine down to the last minute because he caught a bus to his school, a private school, and always left home before his brother did.

Prior to locking up the house, Stem grabbed Sam, who was a small stray dog he adopted the week before, and placed him in the laundry with caged budgies for company. Yard maintenance was not his father's strong point, and Stem didn't want his new canine friend to slip through a makeshift barrier. After placing newspaper down on the tiles, Stem gave the dog some dry biscuits and a bowl of water before heading to school. He joined the slow trickle of children dragging their feet through his street. The fog was thinning, and the sun had begun to melt the patches of ice on the grass along the footpath. His winged friend was nowhere in sight.

Upon his entrance through the school gates, Stem walked through a group of boys, who were in awe of a classmate's time of arrival that morning. He reached for his school bag from under the building feeling defeated, and then stood in the circle of youth until he was noticed.

'This is dumb,' he said, before heading off towards a group of kids less popular.

At the end of this rough day at school, the child came home to an empty house. As soon as he laid eyes on the property, he felt a heavy sense of sadness and his chest tightened for no apparent reason. He unlocked the door. It was quiet, too quiet. He moved through the kitchen and into the laundry.

'No, no, no!' he cried.

Sam, the stray dog, stood silent and still amongst decapitated budgies. He had destroyed the cage and mutilated all five of the defenceless creatures. This was a really dark day for a kid who just wanted his pets to have some company and to be noticed from the outside in. He was growing up too fast, and the lessons he was learning were coming at him with no sign of slowing down.

Without tears, instinct took hold. He knew deep down that the dog was not to blame, nor his brother or parents. It came down to him and his decisions, and how he saw the world; not how the world saw him. Stem was confronted with a situation and the only thing he could do was act like an adult when no adults were present.

In his mind, without any formal training in these kinds of situations, nothing could be done in the slaughterhouse except free the dog and make sure it understood never to come back. Stem cleaned up the bloody mess before the others got home and waited for retribution. It disturbed him greatly that he had allowed such cruelty to take place. Despite being openly devastated, his parents handed down no punishment; he was obviously working things out himself, they figured. Sam never did return from the creek tracks.

On that tragic day, news came in that Grandma Olga, who seemed to have the deepest affection for Stem, passed away.

Over the ensuing weeks, particularly in the classroom, dizzy episodes, an apprehension of impending doom, and paranoia became the norm. Sheer terror consumed Stem as he suffered silently for a time until he couldn't contain his feelings anymore. His childhood was completely interrupted, and he could no longer hide that which needed to come out.

Stem's parents took their son to the best medical doctors they could find. The conclusion that these doctors came up with was identical. They put it down to childhood anxiety. They suggested medication, but one trial of that actually made matters worse and his parents refused to continue down that road.

After Bliss and I heard Stem's story, we reinforced the knowing that his brother and parents were looking out for him despite their behaviours and situations. He had to trust that people had busy lives and other distractions, just as he did in his phase of maturing. I told him that whenever a crow made an appearance, to see it as a reminder that it was neither here nor there what other people thought about him.

'Crows are intelligent creatures that can adapt in many different environments,' I explained. 'You are a very bright person and you are being reminded that you cannot control every situation; however, you can adapt in all of them and learn from each experience. This is the stuff that makes a great human being even greater. Embrace the changes and don't be afraid of falling every now and then. Falling is not the same as failing. All these things are experiences and make up a small part of something much larger.'

Stem will be able to recognise things more clearly when he gets older, but only if he keeps his mind open to these kinds of incidents and their deeper meanings. Just like the budgies in his care, he too feels as though his wings are clipped and he lives in a cage, not a home. His isolation has made him feel vulnerable and displaced.

'Some people see with their eyes and others see with their mind,' Bliss explained. Stem's face lit up, as if he had heard sound for the first time in his life. 'The ones who see with their eyes are what we call followers. The ones who see with their mind are called visionaries. It is the visionaries that usually lead a fuller life and contribute more to society. I encourage you to explore your mind, Stem, your beautiful and perfect brain. Decorate it however you want, because it is your home.'

That was Bliss talking and I was in awe. I could replay those words over and over again from that session. She not only gave Stem permission to be his own person, but she also gave me and you the keys to our own destiny. I knew she shifted something inside me because I no longer felt like playing this doctor/patient game. I wanted to remove the past and settle into the simple things in life, like planting a tree, taking a photograph of a sunrise and making my bed.

Stem will be alright, I know he will. He has asked to see Bliss for another appointment and I couldn't be happier for him. I wish someone like her was around during my years of confusion.

I'm showing signs of logical exhaustion. Bliss is really concerned about me, both as a friend and colleague. I love her. I really do. So what did I create when I found this out? Drama. I raised 'the two suns' hypothesis, a parallel universe deviation, because I knew it would get under her skin. This is based on a dream she and I shared, literally, but only one of us was willing to acknowledge the significance of it.

'Julian, this must surely be some kind of logical deduction of yours based on the number of bird droppings on the windowsill, or something equally fanatical!'

'Consider it to be another collective consciousness instead, Bliss, and see where it takes you.'

'Julian, I'm aware just as you should be aware, the two suns phenomena proved to be unfounded. What could you possibly gain from dreaming my dreams or revisiting my nightmares?'

'The two suns, or two moons, were a collection of dreams, a flap, but the experiences were still real. Just because we don't fully understand how or why, the phenomenon still took place and there is no reason to block it out.'

'Your riddles are exhausting to process – just talk to me straight and narrow!'

'We have the same friends.'

'I don't know what you're talking about. You're a loner.'

'I'm not alone when I'm by myself, just as Stem is not alone in his loneliness.'

'Please stop, Julian, you're frustrating me and not making sense. You're simply suffering depression and you know how screwed up that becomes if left unchecked.'

'I didn't realise I had this ability to communicate with them until –
'

'What?' Oh no! Julian. Stop. You're special, but c'mon, don't go there again.'

'Actually, we are the aliens, you know; the invaders of harmony and balance.'

'Huh? Who has gotten into you this time? The patients, Ravine Arcane, Father Keith, your inner child? Who, Julian? Who?'

'Damn those human emotions, eh Bliss? So which face did you not recognise in our dream? I know we spoke.'

'Look, if aliens are real, and I'm not ruling it out completely, why haven't we caught one or found solid evidence of their existence?'

'We're talking about multidimensional beings. How does one catch and preserve a shadow, or restrain a vision?'

'This conversation is over, Julian. I have real work to do. Damn it! You think you're so bright you can't even cast a reflection!'

'Tell me, Bliss … such a gentle name, Bliss. How long can you hold your breath whilst holding onto my hand?'

Something in that last comment hit a nerve. The air stopped circulating. Bliss gave me the longest stare, and the floor beneath my feet began to slide. It was during that lifetime I felt Bliss let go of my hand. I became really frightened. I was holding onto Bliss too tightly all along.

An assignment we ignored falls into Bliss's lap and crawls deep inside her. She signed up long ago for the challenges ahead and soon it will be time to deliver a result. Finally the apprenticeship is truly over, and I have really learnt a lot from knowing Bliss.

Her wings stretch out and embrace me. She has powers that I have never felt before from another human being. I hold back the emotions of years of suppression. She pushes even closer to my heart. Bliss has something extra that I do not possess. I begin to recall parts of my life that bring tears to my eyes.

Bliss is a professional of the highest calibre. I have visions that she will delve into the sickest of minds and fire receptors in the most inaccessible regions, to stimulate a healthy response.

Everything, as it always was and will continue to be, is conditional based upon our behaviours. Everything written is perfect on its own and out of place in the rest of the universe. Yes, everything is a mystery, and the mystery is everything.

A woman knows what man cannot; the woman feels what man abuses; the woman sees what the man ignores; the woman is our only lifeline to survival and the man is ignorant of that very fact.

'Julian, I'm pregnant, and I'm keeping it.'

26

blow

Bliss says she is with child. Externally there's no sign of it except for a healthy glow. And here I am, smothering my personal growth whilst a new generation is formed inside nature's laboratory. My world is trivial compared to the complex and wondrous realities of the universe. The land I stand on, the air I breathe, the water I absorb, all have secrets. I'm one of the few patients not making progress, and it might be time to find a cave and let nature take back what belongs to the earth, my dust.

And poor little Judas. He still likes comic books, and I wonder if he will ever advance to more challenging literature. I struggle to get beyond these intellectual observations. My soul doesn't belong to me any longer. I'm detached; a sponge absorbing everyone else's pain and yet choose to ignore their joys. The needy ones nail me for a conclusion, and I feel sorry for them; they use lots of energy smashing through flesh and bones to reach a place of calm and understanding. Using primitive tools such as the human mind can only cause confusion, not enlightenment.

I call upon my childhood to shelter me from adult responsibilities, but only find abandoned memories filtering through. I try again and again to find myself. Within several layers of thought I finally see a light in the shape of a dark being remove my young body from myself and place me in the other world. I was examined and worked on. My eye was removed in one procedure and something was placed near my pineal gland. Yes, the third eye now exists and it has become my window between many worlds. I have biological parents, but I have much greater respect for my extraterrestrial family. I don't know any of them by name, only by their single mindedness.

As an adult I can't face personal truth, even though I stare at it daily. There is much responsibility when carrying the weight of a grown-up. I retreat once again. As a boy I can easily be awake staring at the dancing silhouettes on my wall and imagine the gods of the arctic region bringing me good news. It's a welcoming change from all this heat. I listen attentively and they enlighten me of their travels until logic ruins it for me again. Why must I question the non traditional gods every time? Yet again I convince myself that this is all make-believe because it does not belong in the adult's world of reasoning. The magic is lost along with my childhood.

After our heated conversation, Julian had spent several weeks hidden like a cicada whilst developing his form; a necessary incarnation. As a most ordinary creature without vibrant colours or features, he crawled to a very high place from his burrow and clung to existence. Julian became exhausted and his body casing cracked slowly. This is when his known world disappeared and another one appeared. Simply referred to as 'sleep', this section kept me awake at the most inconvenient times.

The first dream drops me in a small, cold, dark dungeon. I'm alone. I'm alert. Someone's coming up behind me. I'm dead, so I believe, or worse.

The second dream instantly sends me to another familiar situation. I was expecting them when their ships filled our skies. Everyone runs for cover and is panic-stricken. The scale is even too overwhelming for me. I stand in awe and unwarranted fear despite already interacting with them on numerous occasions. I knew this day must come. I'm dead, so I believe, or better.

I'm alive again in familiar surroundings. It's a cool climate; I can smell the high country from inside my stately home. I feel my life is a lonely existence. Conversely, I also feel my life is overcrowded and complete at the same time. The exhaustion I feel is crippling, as I turn to five visitors and tell them to please let me rest this evening. These guests respect my situation and disappear, literally disappear from my living room. I drag my feet towards the back door as I pass the kitchen and lock it. My bedroom is teasingly at the other end of the house. The address is large for one person, but not ridiculously spacious for me because I have many guests passing through my walls constantly.

A young solid stature of a man blocks my path on my way to a bed for which I long. All is not well inside my human brain, and I instantly lower my head and refuse to look at him. I cannot handle this being; I will not allow myself to recognise him despite his unmistakable genetic fingerprint. I scream at the impossible and turn away sharply from the creature. I plead with it to leave me alone. I can handle all sorts of life forms, but this one is far too extreme. This monster reappears everywhere I turn and obstructs my path. He has a genuine need to show me truth in its most pure form. He pleads with me that all is well. The human mind is not capable of processing this much truth. I'm unable to accept his purity. There is not one single living cell in my body that can tolerate an ending like this.

This being stands quiet now, just watching. I can feel his joy, sadness, and frustration. It wants to reach out and embrace me. It wants to show me that some flowers never die. He is held back by the fragile balance of prematurely destroying what he has come to salvage. I notice his arms rise in a gesture of goodwill and I dart a quick glance at his welcoming intent look. My brain violently reacts. One arm lowers and extends towards me, as if offering a hand to a dog to sniff.

'It's okay,' he says gently.

'IT'S NOT FUCKING OKAY!' I scream with worn-out vocal chords.

I feel myself imploding as I search deep within for cover. The more I try to hide the more exposed I seem to be.

'Trust me,' he says. 'It is alright.'

This being has no power to make me calm, only to disturb me beyond my human limitations. My intelligence can take no more, and I collapse on the floor. A part of me is concerned that permanent brain damage from such exposure will be the result. With unparalleled lack of understanding I finally escape. I'm dead, so I believe.

I'm alive again. A thick, clear hose is handed to me by an invisible hand. I hold it. A line of people suddenly appear. I recognise many of them. My reserves are depleted. There is no possible way I can give more blood. I have nothing left. I'm dizzy.

'Please,' the one in front of me pleads, 'I need it badly.'

I'm ill. Still I can never deny anyone even though there is nobody left to give me support. I push on. I draw a huge breath and place the tube in my mouth. I blow. Blood fills the clear tubing and drains my reserves further. I cannot see where the blood goes. A smile forms on a stranger's face, which turns from grey to rosy. I remove the tube and lean my hands on my knees and double over.

'Is that enough?' I ask with bloodied lips splattering.

'Could you just give a little more?'

He eventually walks off with more of my insides, only temporarily satisfied. I'm happy I could help although I dread it will never be enough. I've never known such weightlessness without having an OBE. I don't know how I function at all. I see a grassy place to rest. I don't make it there. Before long there is a line up of people holding thick, clear tubing. I try to accommodate their needs, as if it's my duty to do so. I begin to blow streaming blood into an endless line of hoses. I notice the texture has become watery. Meanwhile, I'm falling deeper into some hypnotic vision. I have escaped again into a dream within a dream within a dream… I'm dead, so I believe.

I'm suddenly talking to an old man. 'Okay,' he agrees, 'I'll do that for you, Julian.' I'm delighted. The gent is about to die in a hospital bed and he is going to offer something to science: his soul. I prepare for his inevitable death. There is nothing left for him in this life, and he is looking forward to retirement. I wait by my primitive-looking apparatus, which is in an adjoining room. I casually sip on my cup of tea as if I was about to read a book.

Old Henry is now slipping away. His body lets go, and I pick up his vague whereabouts on the silvery bed of moving nails, which stands in front of me like a computer monitor. There is also a graph displaying vital information on my right, which changes with every movement of the pins. A button that resembles a metal, decorative, cigarette lighter is in my hand. I press it.

'Henry, can you hear me?'

'Huh?'

'Henry, what do you see?'

'Umm?'

'This is important. Please tell me what you see before you go any further. Remember our agreement?' The pins on the board are moving, and I can make out a vague outline of Henry's face.

'I have to go now,' are his last words.

'Wait! Please tell me what you see!'

The moving pins slide back to their prior positions, and the graph peters out. All transmission is lost. I should be happy because no one has ever accomplished such a scientific evaluation of the afterlife before, but all I feel is shame. How could I do something so invasive to another soul? How could I rob them of the experience just so the people living won't be so afraid to die?

I cannot go on with my research and my next experiment. Betty has to be told. She was disappointed, for it distracted her from the inevitable motions of death. Deep down I knew she wouldn't want such intrusions when her time comes. I destroyed all my records and died, so I believe.

I wake in my stately home dream again, mental and physical exhaustion still destroying my mind and body. I'm lying on my comfy mattress on my side with my back towards the window; night time continues. I don't recall climbing into bed from the kitchen area. I'm paralysed and I feel a presence in my room. I'm too tired to care about strangeness anymore and benefit from the immobility. Someone is behind me.

'Are you ghost or alien?' I'm surprised I can talk during this state of freeze. Although my question was asked, I don't care either way just as long as that other thing I saw near the kitchen keeps its distance. There's no reply. I think ghost, but paralysis doesn't occur with me when a dead one is present. Maybe I'm causing my own immobilisation? I'm too tired to check if I can move my body so I wiggle a toe. I have full freedom of movement, but I'm too spent to react. I feel a gentle touch on my lower leg. It feels like Heaven through silk sheets.

'How I missed you,' I let her know without really comprehending who it is. 'I want to see you.'

Still no sound. The touch of an angel travels up my back.

'I don't have to see you.' I change my mind. 'It's not important. I'm just glad you're here.'

'Julian, you must leave this place,' a female voice says and gives me a set of numbers starting with nine and six digits in all. 'It's no good for your health.'

'I know. I'm just so glad you're here,' I repeat with unreserved love. Her gentle touch makes all that other bad stuff disappear. I fully appreciate that I cannot solely be dependent on her to get me out of trouble, just as others can no longer drain me of such emotions.

'Could you please give me your hand?' I ask. 'I need to hold something of yours.' I sense her reluctance. 'Please, just your hand, that's all,' I plead again.

Something large slips over my neck. I reach for it and pull it forward. It is alien-angelic in appearance. With the smooth, thin hand firmly in my grasp, I move it towards my lips, kissing it repeatedly with slow loving motions. I stop and hold it close to my mouth and breathe on it, releasing all my tension from my mortal state. My alien-come-angel-come-mother-come-lover-come-friend-come-child-come-self has put me soothingly back to sleep. I am no longer dead, so I believe.

Julian woke up as a cicada would. He split open his casing and emerged as a colourful, vibrant creature. He made much noise, for there is much to be said. In this forest he is surrounded by so many others just like him. There are many cicadas rattling the same chorus and competing for attention after a long sleep and transformation.

Future generations depend on sleep paralysis, for it gives way to healing the limitations of the human brain.

How did his incarnation come about? This question only becomes important when there is nothing left to live for, when there is only death to set one free of this encasing we call being awake.

27

illusions of delusions

'Fuck your perceptions of God!'

Well, that's not exactly what he said, but it rings true to me. It's only now that I can speak about this conversation with Jesus because I cannot influence the outcome any longer.

I was a priest at the time when I found Jesus bleeding under my bed. He wasn't alone; I can assure you of that. He's not a tall slender man with long blond hair and baby blue eyes, as portrayed in religious art. Instead, he has a kind face with dark, olive skin and short, dark hair. Jesus and others took refuge from the mob mentality in the homes of those who were questioning their faith. They were retelling a new testament and revealed to me that the holy books are not to be taken literally. I offered to listen to their words at the time, but I had my suspicions. Now I believe them when they speak to me without the assistance of religious teachings to pollute our direct communications.

'Do not follow this one or that one,' one of them said. 'Especially do not follow the one that says "you must not follow any of them except for me", for that one is most certainly misled. There cannot be compromise.'

There are other 'others' with my Prophets. These are not like you, although a little more like me. They are curious and bewildered. They have trouble understanding the human mindset, and I find it difficult explaining it to them.

'The soul of a deeply religious person is like a delicate rose made of glass,' one of them observes. 'It is colourless and odourless and must be handled with extreme care. Your religions are fragile ornaments that have no real value.'

Who talks with such contempt? Do you yearn to know their secrets? Nothing is ever as it seems, my friend. Forgive me; pardon me whilst the multiverse within my shell explains my pain via automatic writing.

Don't flatter yourself, brethren; I am not the product of Satan or other so-called evil entities such as jinn. Your opposing religions are not singled out due to personal hatred. As an individual I'll hold you close to my heart; however, as a collective you had better steer clear because I am only one, not many. I have freewill just as you do, so please spare me the list of conditions you impose on God's Unconditional Love with your man laws.

God is not terrifying, remember, you teach this too. Religion is a destructive disease. All of God's organisations on Earth speak with such authority that people become frightened of a demanding God. What better way to fill worship houses and sustain armies than to incite fear and hatred by using love as a drawcard?

Nobody needs to fight for God for He/She/It is fighting for you in your space of disillusionment.

By my opposition alone I have become an ally of yours – how bizarre – and that of your enemies also. Are you quick to categorise me as ill-informed? There is no place for me as your enemy, and I am certainly not your supporter either. My opinions are valid and they will frighten you. Julian is ill, but is he ill-informed?

Public executions of innocent souls are commonplace amongst many of your kind and yet a word or two about spiritual values sends you lot into a headstrong head-spin. Try to execute the idea that mob mentality is not serving anybody and you will be humbled.

This is history; pay attention for it hasn't happened yet, but it will over Earth time.

Christendom will choke.

With great respect, brothers and sisters, drag Jesus, the said Christ, off the pagan cross hanging from your chocking necks and suck in the poison of reality. You so-called lovers of Christ have many splinters protruding from your second-rate faiths, and your eyes only witness that which your Church accepts as truth. Jesus deserves more than what you offer, and you deserve nothing less than you dish out. There is no joy gagging on one's own vomit. I should know; the aftertaste still lingers inside my detoxifying soul.

Buddhism will starve.

With great respect, obese deity who survives on a grain of rice daily, your metabolism is truly miraculous. You sit there so content whilst your servants pay homage to your peaceful ways. But tell me, how can you gloat whilst your devotees do time and cut their locks? What sort of God smirks amongst the starving ones? I should know; starvation still lingers inside my detoxifying soul.

Islam will curdle.
With great respect to your 'peace be upon him' prophets, my awareness is great too. You may have good intentions, but they are steeped with insecurity. You have one God yet you seem to have many masters. At least one branch of the olive tree is not producing good fruit. The tree of knowledge is dying from within. Surely you are worthy of just as much respect as your founder. Mohammed, peace be upon him, and upon you too. The olive is fermenting. I should know; the bitter taste still lingers inside my detoxifying soul.

Hinduism will fade.
With great respect and confusion, which god should I pray to today? What is on offer at the local marketplace? Do you have that one in bronze? Which god can I buy to rid myself of all other gods? There is a production line of entities and yet none of them can satisfy all my needs. Why? Do I ask for too much wisdom, protection, and love? Kissing idols leaves my mouth gritty. I should know; the ashes still linger inside my detoxifying soul.

Judaism will suffer.
With great respect, Mary the mother of Christ was Jewish, and Hitler, the son of darkness, was ignorant. Christian Neo Nazis try to tell a different story. Your indifference to Jesus as God has split many hairs. I ask you respectfully, Judaism, the religion of Abraham, what happened to your

code that your faith too has splintered? Some say that your time has run out. I should know; the emptiness still lingers inside my detoxifying soul.

Paganism will crumble.
With great respect, Sunday is the traditional day of worship for pagans and all religions contain paganism. The sun god burns so bright that the early Roman Christians could not keep the original Sabbath integral. The Ten Commandments were altered to accommodate pagans. If your god is the sun or the moon or whatever, then mine ought to be Jupiter. But it's not. You see, Jupiter protects Earth with her invisible outstretched arms and catches most of the missiles thrown from Heaven. It must surely hurt. I should know; the pain still lingers inside my detoxifying soul.

Shinto will pass.
With great respect, the way of the gods has been worshipped through ancestors and nature spirits. It incorporates death as a window to religion. Ancient land dwellers held similar views, as do tribal religions. However, there has been an invasion. Spiritualists of New Age movements have adopted the declining beliefs and disappointment can only be the result when consulting any quasi medium. I should know; the fraud still lingers inside my detoxifying soul.

With respect to you, the individual. Have I not mentioned your faith? Yes, it is there, binding with grains of dirt. There is nothing special to behold in any organisation, religious, political, or otherwise, only paperwork and judgement. The dust will eventually settle, but not before you do.

Did I mention my name is Julian Aquinas Marcus? I am the priest that never prays and the psychiatrist who is slowly finding his mind in other places of concern. I'm sure I no longer exist because I can hear you reading these words behind walls and beyond them too. Just like a people's prophet, I too have the ability to hide behind God in order to justify my own actions.

These wicked things I speak bleed through and I believe these lies.

28

a bookworm turns

From this moment I, Julian, will speak as the third, tenth, thousandth, or even billionth person. I'm an outsider looking in, for I cannot reasonably convey the upheaval I feel inside or the challenges ahead.

City libraries cater for all personality types. Garden enthusiasts flick their green thumbs through leafy periodicals, artists seek inspiration through the Masters, and poets consider alternative prose.

Julian is at one such institution. He's here to pull secret levers leading to covert societies of the occult. At will, he searches through old books, real books that have the acid of fingers and time on their pages, in order to experience profound acceptance. A well-known surreptitious society opens up in front of the educated man; a grunt escapes his throat with contempt.

This fanciful volume speaks of The Knights Templar in such a way that it becomes an insult to an astute scholar. Julian is deeply aware of the underlying facts and deemed it important for you to know some historical notes about The Roman Catholic Inquisition.

In 1099 a band of Christian crusaders captured the city of Jerusalem from the Muslims. The Knights Templar (originally known as the Poor Knights of the Temple) were a military order founded in 1118 by French nobleman Hugues de Payns, and eight other crusaders to protect Christians travelling from Jaffa to the Holy City. The Roman Catholic Church encouraged the Templars to do their work. St Bernard praised them as 'Christ's legal executioners'.

The Templar organisation flourished and banking systems formed. They purchased a great deal of real estate. Within a few years the Templar's church fortresses spread rampant across foreign lands and they gained a fierce reputation. The riches did not last however. 'Christ's legal executioners' were eventually accused of many sins by order of The Roman Catholic Inquisition.

Urinating on the cross and worshipping Satan – who was in the form of a black cat that the Templars kissed under its tail – as well as other forms of abomination were apparently uncovered. Thirty-six Templars were tortured to death in France and a further fifty-four were burnt at the stake in 1310. In 1312 Pope Clement V admitted there was no evidence of sacrilege within the order.

The Templars were just another religion growing in military strength, nothing more, nothing less. Another dark book diverts Julian's attention, and he plonks the Knights' fable aside.

A leathery hardcover volume of the nineteenth century with an interesting motif branded on the face of it mesmerises the wannabe alchemist. But there's no magic performed and the ancient book smells of hide, not of gold.

There is commotion in the library; horrific screams follow.

Julian's umbilical cord is severed. He walks free from his latest find. More loud cries are in the vicinity. He casually passes hysterical patrons running for the exit and enters the epicentre of disturbance in the Self Help section. Julian is confronted by a man brandishing a high-powered weapon. A few remaining patrons utilise this opportunity and crawl away to safety. Julian is drawn closer to the man despite the danger.

'Stay the fuck away!' the profusely sweaty man warns. 'I'll blow your fuck'n head off!'

Julian responds with a steady, haunting tone; his pace inching towards his final moments of madness.

'If you do that then my time will come and yours will stand still,' Julian says.

'I said STOP you crazy fuck!' The gunman takes a step back as Julian takes two more forward. 'I'll do it, I'll fire!'

'Fire? What do you know about such imagery?'

'You really are a nut job,' the desperate man realises. 'Stop, just STOP!'

'Nut job?' Father Julian recites. 'You must mean "Job" of the Hebrew-Aramaic Scriptures. Yes, I've suffered greatly too.'

At less than a metre away from the would-be assailant a red beam is pointed at Julian's forehead. The confused gunman searches for clues only to find a blank expression.

'Suffering? What do you know about suffering?' the gunman says. 'Look at your clothes. You don't know the meaning of the word!' A shower of spittle rains between him and Julian.

'You're not looking close enough,' Julian challenges. 'Your eyes are black and blue, mine are blue too, even though they are brown in colour.'

'What do you want from me? I'm not going to drop my weapon.'

'I can plainly see. That is becoming increasingly obvious, friend.'

'I'm not your friend, idiot!' the gunman says. 'I'm nobody's nothin'. Get it?'

'You're actually *my* something.' Julian stands his ground. 'You see, I need something from you, friend.'

'You're fuck'n retarded; you ought to see someone about that.'

'But you're the one holding the weapon and terrorising people. And to top it all off, you have made no demands. Do you need attention? Have I not given you hope?'

'Just leave me the fuck alone. That's all I want. Zero you can do for me. Nothing I can do for you. So stop fucking with me and piss off!'

Self help books line the shelves all around the U-shaped bay, and the only way out is past Julian, a prospect that terrifies the trapped soul that has lost all sense of direction.

'Kill me,' Julian says in all seriousness. 'I cannot do it myself, so please let me free with one shot to the head.'

'Don't temp me, you lunatic.' The man lifts his elbow to aim straight.

Julian pulls out his reflective sunglasses and covers his eyes, so the gunman can see his own reflection, before easing down onto his knees. He looks up at the weapon, as if he is besotted with the death knell of laser-fire. Julian chains his insanity with the desperate man. The weapon is lowered and Julian opens his mouth. The barrel is inserted. The cold metallic object moves unsteadily and hits a few teeth.

Julian knows that a loss of life is now a certainty as he gazes into the blue pit of lethal despair. In these last moments he feels empathy for the man holding the weapon without real justification. The original motives of either one of them is now lost in translation.

Even in this final stage of life, Julian probes into the mind of a would-be murderer so he can extract as much information as possible before it is finished. Determination to kill is unquestionable now; Julian sees the forces behind the scenes. The aura of an arduous life thrashing around the gunman reveals little hope. Julian can relate. He has found his emotionally disturbed match in many respects. The mind specialist witnessed an empty vessel devoid of hope.

'I'm sorry,' Julian mumbles, clenching a metal lollipop against his teeth. He breathes heavily through his nostrils and waits for closure.

There is no loud explosion from the trigger, only from a shattered skull, and a body collapses heavily onto the floor. Pieces of flying mangled organs splatter on inner child books and breathless affirmations. The power of positive speech holds its tongue.

Julian Aquinas Marcus is covered in sticky human gunk. The ex-priest respectfully gazes skywards and prays that there is a healing centre for this gunman's lost soul.

Julian walks towards the book he put down earlier and picks it up. He then scans it before emerging from the library where disturbed faces await. Sunshine bakes the gunk on his face. Police officers order him to lie on the ground and to place his hands behind his head. Julian shuffles along in a daze and does not fully comprehend the situation. He hears people screaming 'NO NO!' as if they were in another corridor of existence. A couple of zaps later and he is on the ground convulsing. The ambulance service personnel eventually attended to his police wounds, which were taser related. Julian finally speaks when a camera crew push a lens in his face.

'The victim died by his own hand and society pulled the trigger. Hunt down the system, not the victims. Leave me and the corpse out of your senseless witch hunts and simplistic equations,' he says.

29

Absolution

Fittingly, Julian spoke as a third person in A Bookworm Turns. There is something here that needs to be addressed with sensitivity. Julian, the man, is broken and he is no longer available for comment. We had made arrangements long ago that in such an event I, Bliss, would complete his entries.

Some time has passed since I opened the working copy of Bleedthrough for the first time. I was stunned at the depth of personal information that seeped through the pages and his onslaught of thoughts and actions. My university training has taught me to keep it real under any challenging circumstances. This book is detrimental to the mental health industry standards, but that is not always a bad thing.

Out of respect for my colleague and soul friend, I offer you Absolution in the language of Julian Aquinas Marcus, not necessarily the language of a sane individual.

Overwhelming heavy thoughts haunt Julian. He spends time contemplating his next move in a chequered life while Bliss accepts the future of her unborn child in silence. She is somewhat unconcerned by the prospect of being a single mother; she is after all a modern woman and realises that certain types of men can sometimes complicate matters, especially those found leering about in dark nightclubs second-guessing which skirt will fall next for their charm.

Sunday night finally brings minor relief from days of sleepless stupor, and Julian wakes the next morning with no firm commitment in his bones any longer. His personal organiser has no room for responsibilities and the fantasy world around him has finally packed up and abandoned him. He doesn't feel special or in touch with unseen hands of other multi-dimensions today, and his senses have become lethargically numb. It's a struggle to head for work.

After stepping into the staff elevator at Cathedral Haven, the psychiatrist looks at his smart watch. His eyes take a few seconds to make out the numbers. The elevator stops abruptly between floors, and Julian tumbles in the large, empty cubicle. He is unhurt. The lights flicker, and the ascent continues again.

Progressing out into the corridor and snaking his way to the office, a security guard and two nurses rush past him with a medical kit, almost knocking him over. Such activity is a daily occurrence at the overcrowded facility where negotiations and tranquilizers are often used as a first and final solution. Surveillance monitors are everywhere and nothing goes unnoticed in this chaotically controlled environment.

Mrs Jones, the receptionist, is on phone-cam with an outside caller. Julian waves good morning, but the woman is oblivious to his presence as she brings up files on the screen. Upon entering his office Julian is immediately drawn to a suited man sitting on the patient's lounge. He is unaware of any scheduled bookings this early in the day.

'Did my receptionist let you in?' Julian asks. The man rises to his feet.

'The lady out front, Mrs Jones, yes,' the stranger acknowledges. 'You don't mind, do you, Professor Marcus?'

'No not at all. Sorry I'm late. Were you waiting long Mr...?' Julian reaches for a name in his confusion.

'Gehenna Zenith, and it's never a long wait.' Along with his unusual name, the man had an unusual accent too. 'In fact your timing is perfect.' Gehenna extends his arm and offers a courteous handshake. His hands are covered in smooth leathery gloves. 'What about you? Was it a long wait for you, Professor Marcus?'

'I just got here, Mr Zenith.'

'Yes, of course. As you can plainly see I'm here for a reason.'

'That may be true, but I have none of your files. Which Doctor referred you to me, Mr. Zenith?'

'I believe it was you that beseeched me, Father Julian.'

Julian takes the stranger's religious reference lightly; he's not easily spooked or intimidated by a patient. The one thing that Julian cannot escape though is the familiarity of the gentleman. Moreover, his name screams with powerful overtones. He recalls the meaning of the word Gehenna in the New Testament Scriptures – Hell, a place of torment and suffering. Julian also realises another variant of an actual place; originally the valley of Hinnom, close to Jerusalem, where children were often sacrificed. Zenith is also a term commonly understood. It is the part of the celestial sphere directly above an observer. Some might also say it means the highest point in an individual's fortunes.

'There's no conflicting language within my name,' the stranger says. 'What better way to experience the glory of light than to stand in darkness; and what better way to become part of that glory than to hover high enough that you become part of the light yourself, and then use it to illuminate the path for others to follow?'

'How did you know I was thinking about your name?'

'By using the same technique you utilise. Observation and formulation. I don't need a degree to work things out nor do I have to be a mind reader to interpret your thoughts.'

Gehenna Zenith fogs the air with rebuking style.

'You are an ex-priest who deals with all manner of psychosis. You want to bring down religion due to ignorance and yet you remain in a cloudy space yourself. Of course you would easily recognise my name as something of a curiosity; a contradiction.'

The man sits back on the couch. Julian struggles to put the pieces together. His thought processes are quickly becoming flatter.

'Are you a patient?' Julian asks loosely before realising that his approach is one a hack would use. 'How can I be of service to you, Mr Zenith?' he rephrases.

'By hearing me out without fear or judgment,' he says. 'Do you think you could do that for me, Father?'

'Yes, absolutely, but I am no longer a priest. I lost that title years ago,' Julian stresses. 'I suspect you already knew that.'

'We are what we once were; we are what we will become also,' the patient says. 'It just is.'

'And everything below and everything above is the same; and everything is cyclic,' Julian recalls from Ravine Arcane's notes, referring to the swastika symbol and those found in some alien contact readings.

'No, not quite, Father,' Gehenna Zenith articulates. 'Not from my perspective. After all, how does one compare a hole in the ground to a fire in the sky?'

'Meteors make holes on impact, therefore they are one of the same.' Julian answers almost involuntarily.

'You're not like the others, Julian,' he comments, which is the same line Sandy the homeless man once used. 'We look beyond the obvious, don't we, me and you?'

'Others? We? Tell me about that, Mr Zenith.'

'Other personalities. Other alter egos. Others. We, as in a collective.'

'How do you make such observations?' Julian asks.

'Simply because I have tasted the earth, bathed in the salty sea, and soared through the heavens on prevailing winds.'

'A bit of an adventurer and poet, are you?' Julian quips.

'Absolutely, Julian,' the fellow acknowledges. 'Aren't we all seeking something beyond ourselves?' Julian is slow to respond. Eventually he does so with a nod. 'How far do you go in experiencing life beyond your limit of understanding?'

'I'm here to help you so perhaps my private life should remain just that, private.'

'You are a public servant of sorts, are you not?'

'I suppose in some ways,' Julian agrees half-heartedly.

'As a public servant you are employed by the public. You have personal information about your customers so it is only logical to surrender some of your private information to those who pay your wages, is it not?'

Julian is losing more logic by the second. These words that are debatable have a power all unto themselves. He feels like his brain is starved of oxygen and surrenders to anything half-baked that is put forward.

'What do you want from me?'

'Like I said earlier, Julian, hear me out without fear or judgment.'

'I'm listening.'

'That's a good start, but remember I'm the one who's asking!' Mr Zenith replies in no uncertain terms. 'To what lengths would you go for wisdom?'

'I believe I have already reached the limits in my lifetime. I have sacrificed everything, and you are correct, I still live in the bubble,' Julian concedes. 'Is this what you want from me, a confession? I hope it helps.'

'I don't need such superficial things, Father.'

'Why do you keep referring to me as Father and Julian?'

'Because it is something you need to overcome.'

'I have overcome it and I despise the title Father if you must know. I hate everything that I did in that time when I was one of the chosen,' Julian vents.

'You are still bitter about it and that is why you need to overcome it,' Gehenna reasons. 'Didn't that period in your life teach you any valuable lessons?'

Julian steps into the darkness for a moment and recalls the light at the time. 'Are you? No, you can't be G?'

'No, I'm clearly not your old beach prophet G,' Gehenna sets straight. 'But you are feeling the experience of that turning point in your career and life.'

'How do you know about G then?'

'You're a public servant, remember? You work for me and I have all your records.' Gehenna continues to twist common law with spiritual conquests. 'Now tell me, Julian, why do you show animosity towards the clergy?'

'Have you seen the destruction they have caused? Since when is it a sin to identify wrongdoings?'

'There is no such thing as original sin, as you well know. You still live in a vacuum and you can only identify with the things within your own sphere,' Gehenna states. 'Do you know why you can't focus beyond its curvature?'

'Simple, because I'm powerless to change a corrupt system of denial in all faiths.'

'That's incorrect, Julian.'

'How can that be wrong? I know what I'm feeling.'

'That is part of the problem, feelings. You are occupying the same bubble of prejudice as those that trespass over you. You are all scratching the lens of opportunity at the same time.' Zenith wants to clear matters up and expresses a solution to an age-old problem. 'Can't you see that the way to destroy corruption is to make certain that there is no corruption within yourself first; to make clear acknowledgment of your shortcomings to both the uncorrupted and corrupted?'

Julian's life is transported into another dark place. A level surface where he feels vulnerable; where fear attacks fear with fear. The sudden realisation of this brings him into the dim light of this conversation once more.

'Who are you, really?' Julian asks wearily. This stranger is swallowing all the oxygen in the room.

'You still don't recognise me?'

'No, should I?'

'You will. You didn't recognise me in your dreams either, yet you recognised the others,' he reveals hauntingly. 'Bliss Stone has done well, and you ought to be proud of her.' This latest statement brings Bliss and her unborn child to Julian's thoughts. 'The child is special,' explains Zenith. 'Mother and child are going to do a great service for the future caretakers of this planet. They will continue what you and I cannot complete.'

'Who are you?'

'I'm your closest friend' enters Julian's mind as his ears save vital energy and become impaired. 'Come, let's take another look at the puzzle' also bleeds through.

Without protest, Julian finds himself being led through his office door and beyond Mrs Jones' empty post. The whole department is devoid of people. Julian is unconcerned with such triviality and follows his companion towards the staff area. Next to the coffee machine, people stand silently clutching their warm cups for comfort. All missing persons are accounted for, motionless and silent in this surreal portrait. Julian gradually finds himself near the elevator shaft where medics are working on a body. He pushes through the white cloaks with urgency.

'Recognise me now?' Gehenna Zenith asks. Julian ignores the voice as his human compassion is drawn to a man lying on the ground receiving heart jolts. Julian moves in closer, but is accosted by his patient/therapist/antagonist. 'Recognise me now!'

Julian is finally in sight of the body.

'Julian Aquinas Marcus. Official time of death: eleventh minute, ninth hour, eleventh day of June 2058. Suspected aneurysm.'

Professor Father Julian Aquinas Marcus is alert. He finally recognises himself. He is that monster in the stately home that he could not face. Now, in this instant he is also part of a collective consciousness, part of your choices and his own at the same time. He has burst through the veil and is looking from the outside in, rather than the inside out. He sees that he was never an outsider; it just felt like it. We are all one and the same. There are others with him now, and he recognises all of them too. That Nordic fellow from his strange dream approaches him.

'You have done well,' he says. 'You mortally outlived most of the others that were capable of Bleedthrough and you certainly had lethal doses.'

'Are you dead too?' Julian asks.

'No. And neither are you, just yet,' the teacher replies, 'but it is very close now.'

A wormhole of light is expanding slowly, and Julian regains more life than he has ever known. 'I don't understand. I feel increasingly vibrant, not listless.'

'The unmatched power of your very own Grace and the breath of unlimited Love from your inception will give you all you ever need to survive beyond the physical world,' the teacher explains.

Known dead ancestors stand silently whilst radiating peace and sincere joy. A sudden imprint of understanding comes to the surface; certain extraterrestrial beings of a multidimensional form can mingle with the deceased. These upper echelons are a product of angelic evolution, not crossbreeding.

'Are you not part of this crossing-over process?' Julian directs his question to the teacher as the light intensifies.

'We are all beings created by the same Most Holy, but it is not my time yet. My kind has a greater lifespan than that of the human populace. We have evolved into something less primitive over generations. My particular race has experienced the condition known as "hell" first hand and has been given a taste of the Loving Power that only our Maker can offer too. Your time is now and you will enter the known Unknown.'

'What about my work?' he asks.

'Don't concern yourself; your time is finished. Bliss Stone is a capable young woman. We will guide her to publish Bleedthrough. The mind centre you started is in capable hands, and many young professionals are already subliminally trained to become part of the fresh team under Bliss Stone's guidance. She will pick the right staff and you will be observing her progress indirectly.'

'What about her baby? How will she cope?'

'Like any caregiver with a healthy responsibility and uncompromising support would,' he says.

'So the Bleedthrough diaries were –'

'Bliss makes your work, our work, accountable. Like I said to you some time ago, "all you need to do is observe and record". It wasn't so challenging after all, was it? There will be more to come. That's the way universe works. You have experienced it before.'

Julian slowly loses sight of his physical identity, his carcass left behind in the elevator shaft stuck between floors. Another realisation is present. The blind will see and the mentally ill will accomplish. The ex-priest pours his heart out to those still living. Absolution wraps his soul in a sympathetic embrace of purity, devoid of human illusions and delusions. The mother of all mothers heals his wounds and delivers the final kiss.

Impossible love; impossible words; impossible shapes; impossible textures. Impossible to describe what happens next.

The sick man who once wanted to change the world and make it a better place has made progress. He has regained his memory of what he is as a collective and who he is as an individual. He has finally risen without falling. His former existence is as insidious as a fairytale with a happy ending. Fairytales don't have to make sense; they just require elements of truth, imagination, and hope.

The former things have indeed passed away and in their place stand possible realities; the before-life and afterlife; that never-ending transition from ignorance to universal understanding.

Julian Aquinas Marcus' conscience alone has cleared him of any wrongdoing; not a judgmental God invented from the shackles of

Scripture, but from a real place of belonging to the self and honouring the self before all others.

JAM is what people do together to create new tunes.

JAM is painful, especially on fingers and toes.

JAM is being stuck in a rut.

JAM is to cause interference.

JAM is pleasantly sweet on toast and sickly on its own.

JAM is simply an acronym for Julian Aquinas Marcus.

About the Author

Goran Zivanovic arrived on the Gold Coast at age 11 and still resides there today with his wife, Clare. His earlier childhood in Sydney's western suburbs was somewhat traumatic. This is when Goran first stared to experience the heaviness of being a human, and the want to be something less primitive. Strange encounters and deeply challenging situations gave him a sense of awareness that nobody could relate to in his immediate circle of friends and family. He learned quickly that adults did not know everything. His anxiety was not caused by 'growing pains', as the 'best doctors' informed his parents, they were a result of a closed-minded society.

Goran's parents were not religious, but they took him and his brother to a Christian church at least twice a year to appease other family members. Even from this young age, Goran could see and feel the hypocrisy of all religions and he would react accordingly. There was a deep anti connection, as if he'd been primed by a covert force to only observe and not get infected by the limitations of non secular beliefs.

Later, he would involuntarily get caught up in the sticky web of faith and it became the ultimate survival challenge. An opportunity of death came during his most mind-fucked state when he was struck by lightning at age 33. During the near death experience (NDE) he was free again to clear his mind, his life and all the garbage people believe in, but Goran couldn't let go entirely. He was spoken to by someone or something unseen, but ever present. This entity seemed to give Goran a higher understanding of the often misused term, 'free will'. The mental, spiritual, personal and physical challenges continued without immediate relief. Even after publishing his first book under a pseudonym, Goran felt he was nowhere near satisfied when it hit the shelves. It too became something created from insecurities and ego. However, something changed. It was after the lightning strike that sleep paralysis took hold and his childhood shadow people came out of the shadows.

Eventually, these 'growing pains' stopped hurting. Intelligent bilateral communication became portals where information moves beyond words and into the experiences of Goran's alter ego, Julian Aquinas Marcus.

Psychological realism is Goran's native writing style, because it's less emotionally shielded than other genres. Inspiration always begins with limitations and it's this perspective that forms the blueprint for all of Goran's literary and visual arts pieces.

Gothic Zen Studios is a small film production house in Australia that was established by Goran and Clare. One of Goran's passions is to inspire others to explore the limitless worlds of expression through literature and digital storytelling, without fear or judgement.

Not Enough Acupuncture?

Look for the sequel, *Acupuncture of The Mind, Room 31,* which is based on actual experiences expressed by Julian in true 'Bleedthrough' frequencies and mind-bending style.

Did you like Acupuncture of The Mind?

PLEASE *leave a review on your favourite bookseller's site, or social media platforms, and allow others to benefit from your reading experience.*

So, where to now? Follow Julian's journey and stay updated with his latest offerings by using some of these sites listed below.

Author Website: AcupunctureOfTheMind.com
Film Production: GothicZenStudios.com.au

Amazon.com/author/goranzivanovic
Goodreads @ Goran_Zivanovic
Wattpad @ GothicZenStudios
Medium @ GothicZen

Instagram @ AcupunctureOfTheMind
Facebook @ AcupunctureOfTheMind
Twitter @ EmotiveWriter

www.ingramcontent.com/pod-product-compliance
Lightning Source LLC
Chambersburg PA
CBHW021425110726
47901CB00008B/2304